Kittens and Kisses
at the Cat Café

Kittens and Kisses at the Cat Café

a Furrever Friends Sweet Romance

by Kris Bock

Pig River Press
9781673588484

Chapter 1

Adam let himself into the Furrever Friends Cat Café at 6:30 in the morning. He had half an hour until the café opened, an hour until he had to head to his job. It made sense to come to the café early, when his best friend, Kari, wouldn't need her office. When he wouldn't have the evening distractions of café employees, and customers playing with cats.

That's why he arrived so early. It had nothing to do with Marley, singing a folk song in the kitchen as she started the day's baking.

If you couldn't lie to yourself, who could you lie to?

He paused in the hallway that led between the cat room on the right and the kitchen on the left. The interior windows on the right offered a view into the cat room. Cats sprawled on the padded benches and chairs or peeked out of hammocks and cat tower boxes. He smiled at the sight.

He turned to the left and paused at the counter where they served food and drinks. In the kitchen behind the serving area, Marley kneaded dough. She didn't look up. She must not have heard him come in.

Should he announce his presence? At this point, he'd likely startle her by saying something. He forced his feet to move down the hall to the office. He wasn't there to gawk. He had to figure out their Internet problem.

He indulged himself by leaving the office door open so he could still hear Marley sing. That wasn't creepy, right? She sang even when she knew people were listening, sometimes. He recognized her current song, "Big Rock Candy Mountain," as one she sang to her son.

She had an amazing voice. She'd taken lessons, back when they were all kids. Well, when he and Kari were kids, and Marley was a teenager, the beautiful, free-spirited, kind older girl who treated him like a little brother. Despite their five-year age difference, he'd never seen her as a sister. At first, he'd been in awe of her. Later … that was another matter.

She went silent. Adam paused, looking up toward the doorway, his heart speeding merely at the thought she might appear. A moment later, she started a new song. "Crying Time Again," which he only recognized because Marley had introduced him to so many of those old musicians. The song had a great beat that made even Adam want to move, but the lyrics were sad, about crying because your lover left.

Did she think about the lover who'd left her, after getting her pregnant? She seemed so cheerful most of the time, never complaining. Her son, Brian, was now nine years old, and her whole family adored him. But sometimes, like when she sang, he sensed sadness.

Too bad she'd never been able to do anything with her singing. She'd given up those dreams when she got pregnant at 18 and decided to keep the baby. Maybe that's why she sang sad songs. Maybe she missed her lost dreams, not the jerk who'd left.

Fixing the Internet was easy, simply a matter of a loose cable. Still he didn't leave. It wasn't so bad if he sat in the back office listening to her, right? What else was he going to do with the extra time before he had to leave for work? If he sat back, closed his eyes, and appreciated her voice, who did it hurt?

No one except him, as he filled with the pain of wanting her, loving her, and doubting she'd ever see him that way.

Bang, bang, bang!

Adam jumped about a foot, and Marley's song cut off.

Heart thudding, he pushed out of the chair and ran to the office door. He swung around the doorframe and started down the hallway.

The kitchen door swung open. Marley rushed out.

Adam jerked back so he didn't slam into her.

2

She shrieked and jumped, bouncing off the doorframe.

"Sorry, sorry!" Adam held up his hands. "It's just me." Darn it, he should have told her he was there. Of course she'd be scared when someone pounded on the door, and he appeared out of nowhere. "Are you hurt?" He lifted a hand to check her arm for bruises but couldn't close the last few inches to touch her.

Marley let out a weak laugh and pressed her palm to her chest. "All right, I'm okay, only startled. Why didn't you let me know you came in? I would've given you coffee, and a cherry scone when they're ready. I'm trying a new recipe."

He stuck his hands in his pockets and hunched his shoulders. "That's okay, I don't need anything."

"Mom would say you could use some fattening up." She gave him a playful pinch on his lower rib cage.

Adam snorted out a laugh.

He couldn't think of anything to say. The moment grew awkward.

Marley shook herself. "Right, the door. I almost forgot what startled me the first time. We don't open for another ten minutes. I don't understand why whoever it is couldn't wait. Nobody needs coffee *that* badly."

Marley strode to the front door. She pushed it open, glanced around, and looked down. "Oh."

"What is it?" He couldn't see past her, but something in her voice made him want to drag her back, get out front, and protect her.

She opened the door wider, moving with it so he could see.

He looked down at a cardboard box filled with wriggling fur. "Kittens?"

Marley crouched, propping the door open with her hip. "Five of them. oh, they're adorable."

Adam went down on one knee beside her. One kitten was black, another black and white. One was white with specks of tan. The fourth had a brown pattern, while the

3

fifth had orange and white swirls.

Adam scanned the area for any people. A couple of cars drove down the street. Someone from another business brought out the trash. Whoever had left the box had disappeared. In a car, they could be blocks away.

"They're gone," he said. "I guess they figured leaving kittens at a cat café was like leaving a baby on the doorstep of an orphanage."

Marley stroked her finger over one tiny head. "But it's not. We can't even take them inside. All the cats here have had their vaccinations, but we don't know anything about these. They're so tiny, surely they shouldn't be away from their mother yet."

That would hit her hard. She adored her son with a fierceness that amazed him. Adam hadn't understood her decision to keep the baby at first. After all, he'd only been 13, and having a baby seemed like giving up the rest of your life. But when he saw her in the hospital, holding that baby, everything changed. She'd created new life and dedicated herself to its care. She'd been plump with the baby weight, her hair tangled from the hours of labor, her face pale with fatigue, and yet she glowed with joy.

That was the day he went from having a crush to falling in love.

She didn't know that, of course. Adam had never even told Kari, and as clever as his best friend was, he didn't think she had the slightest idea of how he felt about her older sister.

He sometimes thought Marley and Kari's mother, Diane, had her suspicions. But she never said anything. She probably assumed it was still puppy love. But he was 24 now. Four and a half years was a gulf when you were 13 and 18. Not so much at 24 and 28.

But would Marley ever see him as anything besides her younger sister's best friend, the neighbor kid, her adopted little brother?

4

Marley looked up at him, her brown eyes luminous. "What are we going to do? I'm supposed to open in a few minutes. We can't bring them inside. We can't leave them here. They're so young."

When he was 13, he'd imagined slaying dragons for her. At 15, he'd pictured himself defending her from a gang of muggers. By 17, the daydreams had gotten slightly more realistic. He might pull her back before she stepped in the path of a speeding car. He might rescue Brian from drowning or choking, or find him in the woods when he'd wandered off. It didn't matter that they didn't have a forest within two miles. Adam simply wanted to be Marley's hero. He'd been waiting for the chance. He could certainly take care of this little problem.

"I'll deal with it."

She frowned. Apparently she needed more than a vague promise.

"I'll take them to the vet, the one who works with the shelter," he added. "That's the best place for them now, right? She can tell us what they need, where they should go."

"Yes, of course. It's a good plan." She touched his arm. "Thank you. I'm glad you're here."

He grabbed the box and stood. "Me too. You take care of opening the café. I'll take care of these guys. Then I have to go to work, but I'll text you later, let you know what the vet says."

"Please do." She gave him the smile that made his insides feel like rainbows and butterflies, all mashed together into pudding. "Thanks."

"Of course. Tell Kari I did the thing. The Internet thing. I fixed it."

"What would we do without you?" The twinkle in her eyes now told him she was teasing.

It stopped him from adding, *You never have to find out. I'll always be here for you.*

5

Chapter 2

Marley watched Adam stride down the sidewalk with the box of kittens. He was such a good friend. Always there if her family needed anything.

He must have passed an alley in line with the rising sun, because for a moment golden light splashed across his shoulders and turned his brown hair the color of honey.

Marley blinked rapidly and shook her head. In that moment, Adam had seemed to be someone else, someone grown up and handsome. He'd been such a scrawny, goofy kid. As a teenager, he'd shot up to six feet tall, so skinny you could see his ribs. They'd joked that you could see his liver.

He was still thin, but somewhere along the way, his shoulders had broadened, and she'd felt muscles when she'd pinched him earlier. He had a swimmer's build, long and lean, though as far as she knew, he'd never been a swimmer.

She forgot, sometimes, that he wasn't still that scrawny, goofy kid.

Her watch buzzed against her wrist. Marley shook herself out of her thoughts. She'd burned apple tarts on the day they had the first cats delivered. Granted, she'd had plenty of distractions, with the crowd of people and all the cats, one of them yowling like a siren. But ever since then, she set an alarm on her watch, in case she couldn't hear the kitchen timer.

Marley turned toward the door. From the corner of her vision, a woman approached. Their first customer? Marley glanced toward her.

"Sorry I'm late."

Marley took a closer look. "Holly? Sorry, I didn't recognize you."

Holly's lips, usually painted black, were crimson today.

Her hair was completely covered in a soft hat of the same color. Maybe she hadn't had time to dye it – Marley had noticed the dark brown roots as the black grew out.

"It's fine." The corners of Holly's mouth curved slightly upward, but the smile didn't reveal teeth or reach her eyes.

"You okay?"

"Fine." Holly turned to the door in a gesture that clearly said, *Let's go, and don't ask questions.*

Meanwhile, Marley had scones to save. She hurried on ahead, calling back, "Turn the sign, please!"

She pulled the baking pan out of the oven and set it on a wire rack. A quick check with a toothpick confirmed the scones were ready. Maybe a touch browner than she'd prefer, but not too bad. She'd cool them for five minutes before taking them off the pan.

Five minutes hardly gave her time to do anything practical. Holly didn't seem inclined to conversation as she finished the opening procedures. So Marley leaned against the counter and wondered about Adam.

He was such a cutie. Not to mention incredibly smart, and a real sweetheart. Adam and Kari had been best friends since childhood. Marley would never suggest that women and men couldn't be only friends, but everyone had assumed that Adam and Kari would someday become a couple. Why wouldn't you want to add romance to a wonderful friendship?

On the other hand, there was Colin. He'd walked into the cat café while they were still working on renovations, two years after he'd been badly injured in a war zone. He was a baker, like Marley. He was kind and sexy. Kari had tried to set up Marley and Colin. That plan had utterly failed, which was to Kari's own benefit, since Kari and Colin were now a happy couple.

Marley had felt an immediate connection to Colin, but no romantic spark. He was a brother from another mother.

That must be what Kari and Adam had.

She grabbed a pot holder, lifted the baking pan, and slid the scones onto the wire rack.

The first customer came in. They had been open a few weeks, and still Marley got a giddy sense of relief when actual customers actually came in!

Holly stepped to the counter to take the man's order. Now her smile was in place. The barista didn't share much about herself, but she had a way with people. She seemed to know who wanted to chat, who would appreciate a little light flirting, and who simply wanted to get their order and pay with minimal fuss. Marley envied those skills, especially Holly's ability to flirt while maintaining boundaries. She got asked for her phone number regularly, by both men and women, and whether she gave it or not, she sent the customer away smiling.

Marley had barely dated since she'd gotten pregnant with her son, a decade ago. A decade! Talk about a dating drought. But it was next to impossible when you had a baby, or even a toddler, and then she worried so much about introducing a new man into Brian's life, and after so many years without dating, how did you get started, let alone find someone who would want to date a woman with a child?

Excuses. Always excuses. But the fact was, she dated less than anyone except … well, Adam. Marley had never heard of him dating, though she couldn't claim to know everything he did, especially in college. But he'd certainly never mentioned anyone, let alone introduced a girlfriend, or a boyfriend. She thought if he were gay, he would feel comfortable enough to come out to her family, but maybe he was asexual and simply didn't feel sexual attraction of any kind.

Although once in a while, Marley got a vibe from him …

Holly grabbed tongs and popped one of the scones onto a plate.

8

"Wait, it's a new recipe, I haven't tested them yet!"

Holly gave her a firm stare. "They'll be amazing." She turned to the customer. "Fresh out of the oven. You're the first one to try it. Let us know what you think."

The man grinned and shoved a bill into the tip jar. Was that a five? He turned away clutching his plate like a little boy with the latest issue of his favorite comic.

Holly turned to Marley with a smirk.

"Okay, okay, you know your business."

Holly nodded, put another scone on a plate, and set it aside, at the back of the counter.

"Claiming yours for later?" Marley asked.

"It's for Zack. You know, the guy with cancer who comes in every day."

"Who? Wait, you mean the guy who looks like he's lost weight – he has cancer?"

"Well, yeah."

"He told you that?"

Holly shrugged. "People tell me things. Food tastes weird with the chemo, like this week he can't handle chocolate at all, but I think the cherry scone might work for him." She shrugged again, an indifferent gesture that didn't match her words. "Worth a try anyway."

"Yeah. Good." Marley looked at the scones, the display case, the list of things she had planned to do that morning. "You want to get these set up? I'll check the cat room. I need to move."

Holly nodded and pulled the rack of scones toward the acrylic display case with shelves. They'd gotten the new case so they could keep the baked goods fresh and protected from flies, yet avoid wrapping everything in plastic wrap. Kari was determined to keep the café as environmentally friendly as possible. As a bonus, everything looked fresher and tastier without the plastic film.

Marley hung her apron on a hook. As she went through

the kitchen door, she pulled the elastic band out of her hair. She slid the band around her wrist and ran her fingers through her brown hair to fluff it. In the kitchen, they had to be strict about health code rules. In the cat room, things were more relaxed. When you might have a cat coughing up a hairball on the floor, no one complained if a woman shed a strand of hair.

Their first customer sat on one of the tall stools in the hallway, facing the windows that looked into the cat room. He made a murmur of pleasure as he popped the last piece of warm scone into his mouth.

Some people preferred to eat there, at that narrow counter. They could watch the cats play without worrying about a cat licking their latte. Others preferred to go into the big room and hang out with the cats. The door to the cat room was down the hallway a few feet, so it didn't interfere with the lines at the café counter.

And they really did get lines at some times of day!

Marley paused by the bulletin board they'd installed in the hallway. They wanted to keep the postings to local events or anything related to pets, but sometimes people tried to sneak in other notices. She removed one from someone who had a guitar for sale. She left the notice of the lost dog, which now had a big heart circling the word FOUND on it. Customers who'd worried about the dog would enjoy seeing that.

Another flyer announced a contest: So You Think You Can Sing.

Marley stared at it. Had it been there when she came in that morning? She couldn't remember seeing it.

Now it seemed to speak to her. She loved to sing. Once she'd imagined becoming a famous pop star.

Not anymore. Those dreams had died a long time ago.

Had someone put that flyer there specifically for her? Had Kari, or one of their coworkers, wanted to nudge

Marley into testing herself publicly? Or was it simply a random thing? Marley didn't assume the notice of the medieval dance club was directed at her.

She glanced up and down the hallway. No one was watching her.

She bent to read the details on the flyer. The first contest was at a local bar in a couple of weeks. Basically an open mic night. They'd choose the five best performers for the finals a week after that. The winner got a regular paid gig at the bar, plus a meeting with a music producer.

Marley straightened and tried to shrug away the prickles between her shoulder blades. It was probably a scam. The pub was auditioning potential singers on the cheap. No doubt their "pay" would be collecting tips in exchange for hours of exhausting singing on a weekend night. And the producer would want money to do a demo tape. He'd promise to take it to record companies, and how would you ever know if he did?

It wasn't for her.

She went into the main café room. They didn't have any customers in there this early. It wouldn't be worth opening the café at 7 a.m., except for the steady stream of people who got coffee and baked goods to go. But by midmorning, parents and nannies with children would stop by for a cheap hour or two of entertainment. It had become popular with a few self-employed people, writers and so forth, who liked the chance to get out of the house. Lunchtime would bring a bubble, and evenings were busy, especially when they had events.

For now, Marley had the place to herself. She went into the back room, which held cat beds, food and water dishes, and litter boxes. Even with a litter box for every cat, plus one extra, they had to scoop them several times a day to control smells.

Marley got to work.

This was her life. She sat back on her heels and chuckled. Twenty-eight years old, a single mother, scooping kitty litter on the job. She didn't mind. Working the early shift at the café was better than her previous late nights of waitressing. She didn't get the occasional great tip now, but she had steady income, no slow weeks, and she could spend the afternoons and evenings with her son. It was a good life.

She dreamed of getting a house for her and Brian, nothing big, but with a yard. Then he could have the pets he wanted so badly. She might never save the money to buy a house, but maybe they could rent one. Not this year. Maybe next. For now, living with her mother and sister worked.

She finished scooping and scrubbed her hands at the sink in the back room. She paused to pet Merlin, the big Maine Coon, who sprawled on one of the cat beds. He gave his trilling mew as she scratched his armpit. Many of their original cats had already been adopted. Merlin hadn't found his special person yet.

"It'll happen," Marley whispered.

In the big room, she glanced around for anything that needed doing. Salt and Pepper wrestled on the floor. The two were siblings, one white with black spots and one black with white spots. Autumn, a rare female orange tabby, chirped for attention and purred like a motor when Marley stopped to cuddle her.

So many wonderful cats. But it hadn't been the same since Shadow got adopted. The gray kitten was Brian's favorite. Her son had refused to enter the café since two little girls had taken Shadow home and renamed him Silvertoes.

That reminded her, it was time to text Brian her morning message before he headed to school: *I love you. Have a great day.*

Kari and Marley had agreed – no more kittens at the café. For one thing, they easily got adopted at the shelter.

12

The café should show off adult cats who might not get picked right away. For another, Brian fell in love too easily. He didn't need another broken heart.

He would have loved seeing the kittens that morning. Loved it too much. Just as well he'd been at home with his grandmother.

Her watch signaled a text. Brian? He hadn't been responding to her morning texts lately, and when he did, she had a feeling her mother made him.

Not Brian. Adam. Did she know the vet's name?

She chuckled. He strode off like an avenging warrior, promising to take care of things, and he didn't even know where he was going. What had he been doing for the last 20 minutes, driving aimlessly hoping to find a vet's office?

Silly boy.

Chapter 3

Adam had assured Marley he'd take care of the kittens. Unfortunately, it wasn't quite as simple as he'd made it sound. First he had to figure out who the vet was, the one who worked with the shelter and approved cats as healthy enough to go to the café. He'd assumed the vet worked out of the shelter, but now he wasn't sure. Would an animal shelter really have a vet on staff full time?

He should have asked Marley before he left. He'd been too busy trying to show off to think of practical things. He'd feel foolish asking her now.

At least the shelter could tell him who the vet was, so he drove there.

By the time he arrived, he needed to leave for work. If he had to take the kittens someplace else, he'd be late. Not that they'd fire him for coming in ten minutes late, but he was new; he didn't want to push boundaries.

The shelter didn't open until 10 a.m.

Of course. Who went to an animal shelter early on a weekday morning?

He'd heard the vet's name once or twice. J-something. Julie? Jessica?

No. Jennifer? Closer, but not quite … Jenny! He was almost certain that was it. Somewhat certain anyway. He'd met her at the grand opening, a tall woman in her thirties with long brown hair. Unless that was someone else.

A first name and vague physical description wasn't a lot to go on. He sat in his car and tried an Internet search for a vet named Jenny or Jennifer, but he didn't find what he needed. She might work in a group practice or use initials or he had her name completely wrong.

14

Kari would know, but she worked the evening shift, which went late last night because of a painting party, and then she'd gone home with Colin. They might still be in bed.

He could take the kittens to the office with him.

Some of his coworkers would love seeing kittens, they'd even try to help, but he didn't think his boss would approve of the distraction. Ms. Romano might joke about the kittens not having security clearance, but she'd cross her arms and tap her foot and give him that look that reminded him of his terrifying third-grade teacher.

Mewing came from the box on the passenger-side floor. It wasn't safe to keep driving around with them unsecured. Besides, as Marley had pointed out, they were too young to be away from their mother. They must need food, and he didn't have any. He didn't even know what they needed or how to give it to them. He had to turn them over to someone with more experience.

He sighed. He'd call work and let them know he'd be late.

But first he texted Marley to ask if she knew the vet's name.

It took several minutes for her to respond. She'd had to check Kari's records. The vet's name was Jenna, not Jenny. Marley added the business name, Raining Cats and Dogs Veterinary Clinic. She even included a phone number and address. She ended with a smiley face emoji that seemed to laugh at his incompetence.

Adam called the vet's office and got a recorded message. At least it confirmed they opened at eight and had a walk-in service for emergencies. This sure seemed like an emergency to him. He headed there, arriving at ten minutes before eight.

When a woman with long brown hair got out of a car and crossed the parking lot, he met her at the clinic door.

"Jenna?"

15

She glanced at him and then at the box. He lowered it enough to show the squirming kittens inside.

She sighed. "Let me guess. You got a kitten and thought four months old was too young to have her fixed. Now you have more kittens."

"No. I don't know anything about the mother cat. I was at Furrever Friends when someone dropped off this box. I think we met at the café last month. I'm Adam. Jenna, right?"

She frowned at the box. "You don't have the mother cat?"

"No."

She made a sound in her throat he could only call a growl. "Those kittens can't be more than a week old."

"We were afraid of that." He lifted the box toward her. "Can you take care of them?"

"You live alone?"

"Well, yeah." What did that have to do with anything? "Any pets?"

"No. I've never had a cat." Clearly he was not the right person to take care of five newborn kittens. "You'll take them?"

She opened the door and waved him through. His arms were getting tired, so he lowered the box and went.

"No," she said. "But I'll tell you how to take care of them."

He jerked to a stop in the doorway.

"And yes, I'm Jenna."

He forced himself forward. "I don't know anything about taking care of newborn kittens." He put the box on a counter that cut the room in half. "I have to get to work."

She rounded the counter and turned on a computer. "Me too. I have a packed day ahead. Three surgeries, including a C-section on a bulldog. Unless you want these kittens to die, someone has to feed them every two hours."

16

"Day and night?" Yikes. "For how long?"

"They'll stop when they're full." She sat at the desk and began typing

"I mean how long are they at that feeding interval?"

"It gets longer as they get older. Try to start at two hours now, but this weekend you can lengthen that a bit. In another week, make it three hours."

"Wait a minute, is that three hours starting this coming Monday or the next one?"

"I'll give you a schedule."

He rubbed his hands over his face. "Hang on. You're assuming I'm the one who will be doing all of this. I can't. The shelter, surely they have someone."

"You can try. They can't handle kittens this young at the shelter. They send them out to fosters, if they have any available. But they're overfull and overwhelmed too."

He stared at her helplessly.

Jenna glanced up. "I know. It stinks. But if everybody expects somebody else to take care of the problem, the problem doesn't get solved."

He looked down at the squirming, mewling kittens. They were so little, so fragile. How long could they survive if someone didn't take responsibility?

They wouldn't last the day. He ran his hand through his hair. "You can tell me what to do, right? What they need? Where I can get some, what, cat milk?"

"We have some kitten formula." She gestured toward shelves on the other side of the room. "I'll set you up with everything you need. Since you didn't cause this problem through your own neglect, I'll give you the discount we give the shelter, so the vet work is basically at cost. Call on your friends. Together, you can handle this."

Adam sucked in a breath. Another. He stopped feeling lightheaded. "Yeah. Yeah, we can."

They had to.

17

She stood and smiled at him. "Great. Come on back. We'll get them warmed up and I'll do a quick exam to make sure they don't have health problems." She took the box and walked briskly through a door behind the counter.

Health problems. What if one of them was already sick? Or all of them? He couldn't handle that kind of care.

What if they died? That would be worse.

Jenna put the box on a table, turned on a lamp, and aimed it over the box. The heat reached Adam two feet away.

He glanced around the room. He'd never been in the back of a veterinary office. He couldn't identify half of the equipment.

Jenna grabbed an electric kettle, filled it, plugged it in. She put on a lab coat and a pair of glasses. She examined the first kitten, the all-black one. "Do they have names?"

"No. We haven't even thought of that."

"This one is a boy."

"Okay." Adam turned at a sound behind him. Another woman came through from the front. Jenna gave her a rapid series of orders, and the young woman got busy.

Adam glanced at his watch. He might have to let his boss know he'd be more than an hour late.

Jenna examined the rest of the kittens, identifying one more boy and three girls. "They all look good. No bleeding, no eye infections, no sign of fleas. A bit dehydrated and no doubt very hungry. They should do fine, fingers crossed."

Thank goodness. He'd hate to report anything different to Marley.

"They'll need kitten formula for another three weeks. Then–" She waved a hand in a dismissive gesture. "I'll give you printed instructions on the next steps."

Uh oh. How many steps were there?

Jenna turned to a shelf and grabbed a canister that had a picture of a kitten on the front. "This comes as a liquid or a

18

powder. I recommend the powder. Make it fresh every time." She demonstrated with a scoop, water, and a canning jar. She had Adam shake the jar well while she checked on her assistant.

"You can put the formula in a mug of hot water to warm it up. I use an electric kettle." Jenna poured hot water into a mug and popped in a tea bag. "This one's for me." She filled a larger container half-full. "Hot water, add the jar. Give it about thirty seconds." She bobbed her tea bag in her mug, added sweetener from a small packet.

The formula went into a plastic syringe with a rubber nipple. Jenna squeezed a drop of formula onto her wrist. "It shouldn't feel hot or cold." She pulled the white-and-tan kitten out of the box, placed it on the table, and held it gently by the shoulders with one hand. When she held the bottle angled down in front of the kitten's mouth, it started suckling.

Adam had a powerful urge to take a picture. It was so cute.

Actually, a picture wasn't a bad idea, and video was better. He had to remember how to do this, and he'd have to teach other people if he didn't want this to be his job day and night. He pulled out his phone and started filming.

"Feed them every two hours. No cow's milk. It can kill them. Kitten formula only."

"Got it." Adam stopped the video. It should be enough to jog his memory and train others. He put his phone in his pocket.

"Generally, they'll sleep between feedings," Jenna said. "Make sure they're safe and warm. A box is fine, but you'll want a bigger one so there's no chance one will climb out and crawl away."

It was hard to imagine one of these helpless creatures climbing out of anything at this point, but they'd grow quickly. Thank goodness, or he'd be up all night for much longer.

"Put a heating pad in the bottom," she said. "Keep it on low. Completely cover it with a soft towel or blanket. More soft blankets for them to lie on or snuggle under. Make sure they have the option of staying close to the heat or farther away."

"Hang on, I need to take notes." He pulled his phone out again, opened a notes app, and tried to catch up.

"You'll also need to stimulate the kittens to go to the bathroom. Their mother licks them to stimulate urination and elimination." Jenna glanced up at him and said dryly, "You'll be glad to know we don't expect you to do that."

He managed a weak laugh.

"You have that warm water left over from heating the bottle. Dunk the end of a cloth into it – washcloth, paper towel, toilet paper, but make sure it's soft and you have enough to soak up the urine." She demonstrated, soaking one end of an extra-soft paper towel and dabbing at the kitten for a full minute.

The kitten peed and pooped into the paper towel. Adam took notes.

Jenna tossed the paper towel into the trash. "Dip a clean cloth in the water. Rub it over her face first." She showed him. "This helps teach them to groom themselves properly." She dabbed at the kitten's behind. "Make sure you've cleaned off any feces and urine."

"Okay. I think I get it." Five times. He'd have to do this for five kittens, every two hours. How would he have time for anything else?

"At three weeks old – say, another two weeks from now – put them into a litter box after you feed them. Do this stimulation there. That will help them associate the litter box with going to the bathroom."

"Litter box … bathroom …" Adam muttered as he typed.

"Now you try one."

"Me?" Of course. It made sense. Do this once here, so she could check that he was doing it right. He put his phone away and cautiously picked up the kitten with the orange and white swirls. A girl, if he recalled correctly.

She started suckling at his fingers. Aw. So cute.

Adam put her on the counter, held her as he'd been shown, and offered her the bottle. That part was easy enough. He wished Marley were there. She'd enjoy this. So would Brian.

The peeing and pooping part was a little more awkward and a lot less cute, but he managed it.

Jenna clapped him on the shoulder. "Good job. I officially declare you capable of feeding kittens. Go ahead and feed the other three." She turned away.

Adam glanced around. Another employee had come in, and voices buzzed in the waiting room. How much time had passed?

He had yet to get all the things he needed to take care of the kittens. He had to take them home, get them properly set up, figure out who would feed them while he was at work.

With a sigh, he called his office to say he was taking a vacation day.

And then he went back to feeding kittens.

Jenna stopped by between patients to check on his progress. "You'll bring them back at six weeks for their first vaccinations. Get them spayed or neutered at eight weeks. I know, it sounds young, but don't wait. It's never too early to start searching for appropriate homes for them. Assuming you don't want all five for yourself, that is."

He imagined coming home to five grown cats. He'd heard of people with that many or more, but going from no pets to five all at once sounded like a recipe for disaster.

"Right. Find them homes. Once they're fixed and everything, they could go to the café, right?"

"Sure, assuming they're all healthy. No reason to think otherwise, but we'll check for FIV." She peered into the box and tickled a waving paw. "Normally I'd also encourage you to get the mother fixed; if she's feral, trap and release her, prevent this from happening again."

"No idea where she is."

"Yeah." Jenna sighed. "Keep an eye out for a stray cat in case the mother gave birth in your neighborhood."

"Will do." He nodded a couple of times. His head felt too full. "Please tell me that's everything."

"Hardly." She gave him a sympathetic smile. "But maybe that's enough for now. I printed some literature with links to good websites. They're at the front desk." She headed to an exam room.

Finally he had plump, dozing kittens, canisters of powdered kitten formula, a number of other things he apparently needed, and a bill that made him blink despite the discount.

Adam checked over his notes, confirmed the feeding schedule for the next few weeks, and made another appointment with the receptionist.

He had time to get home before he had to start the next feeding.

Chapter 4

By the time Marley had a break, she wanted coffee and a snack. They'd sold all the scones except the one Holly had put aside for Zack. Marley hadn't even been able to taste one, though she'd been assured they were terrific. With a sigh, she pulled yogurt and a hard-boiled egg out of the fridge. She needed the protein, even if she craved the sweet carbs. Plus, she knew how many calories were in the things she baked. Well, she could guess, based on the ingredients. She'd never had the nerve to do the math.

"I'm taking a break, then I'll tackle cat cleaning." That was how they euphemistically referred to litter box patrol, since "scooping poop" might put customers off their food.

Holly glanced at the clock. They had an hour before it would get busy. "Take your time."

In the big room, Marley glanced around to make sure everyone seemed happy. Two women were deep in conversation, seated on the padded bench with a cat in each of their laps. An older couple had finished their drinks and pushed their chairs back from a table. The woman had a wand with feathers on the end. She made it dance as Salt and Pepper chased it.

A middle-aged man sat at a round table with a coffee drink – a cappuccino, Marley thought, with a smiling cat face swirled into the foam – and their popular sample platter of five baked goods. He popped the piece of lemon bar into his mouth and chewed slowly, his expression thoughtful. His eyes focused on Marley.

She smiled. "I hope you're enjoying everything. Let me know if you have comments. We're always happy to get customer feedback."

He studied her without speaking. Marley shifted awkwardly. Clearly she was not good at identifying who wanted to chat, but he could at least say something. Even "Leave me alone" was better than this silent scrutiny.

She should simply turn away and sit down.

"Do you know who I am?" he asked.

Marley opened and closed her mouth several times before she finally came up with, "No. Should I?"

"Never mind." He looked down at his plate.

Marley stood for a moment, staring at the top of his balding head. He did not look up again. What on earth was that about?

She shook her head and edged toward another table.

He glanced up at her. "The baked goods are adequate."

Adequate? Adequate! She drew in a slow breath and turned away. She marched back through the door and into the kitchen.

She smacked her yogurt on the big prep table. The top popped and a stream of yogurt splattered the table. She put her coffee mug and the hard-boiled egg down more gently before spinning away to pace the room.

"You okay?" Holly asked.

Marley turned to glare at her. "Adequate!"

"Okay?"

Marley pressed fingers to her temples. "Sorry. Not you, obviously. Some guy in there. He said the baked goods were adequate. And he asked if I knew him. Like he's famous or something? And when I didn't, he insulted me."

Holly leaned across the counter to get a better look through the windows into the cat room. "Balding guy, beaky nose? I don't recognize him."

"Because he's nobody! Nobody important." Marley stood with her hands on her hips.

Holly's lips twitched. She pressed them together, clearly trying not to smile.

24

Marley burst out laughing. Holly joined in.

"Okay, I'm overreacting," Marley said. "It's not like everyone in the world must love my baked goods. Still."

"Still, weird," Holly agreed. "I wonder if he is someone famous. Maybe you hurt his feelings first."

"I suppose. He could be a big actor for all I know. I don't watch that many movies without animated characters."

Side by side, they leaned across the counter to study the man. "He looks like he could play an English butler," Holly said. "Did he have a British accent?"

"Maybe?" Marley tried to think back. He hadn't said that much. "Kind of fancy anyway. I'm not good with accents." Why would she be, considering she'd never left her home state? "If he is famous, should we do something about it?"

Holly arched an eyebrow. "Such as? Ruin his career?"

Marley snickered. "No, I mean for the café. Take his picture and get an autograph or something, like some restaurants put on the walls."

"It's going to be awkward if we don't know who he is." Holly put on a fake smile and batted her eyelashes. "Excuse me, sir, can we take a picture of you? And get your signature? Be sure to write legibly, so we'll be able to figure out if you are, in fact, *somebody*."

"Okay, it's a silly idea."

"No, it could be cool to get some famous guy's autograph. If he came here, he must like cats, right? Maybe we could get a photo of him with one of ours. Share it on social media. We might not know who he is, but if other people do, it's publicity for the café. But we need to figure out who he is first."

"How do we do that?"

Holly tapped out a rhythm on the counter while she thought. "Take his picture without him knowing. Then we'll do a reverse image search and see what comes up."

"Will that work?"

"We'll find out if we try it."

They looked at each other for a minute. Marley said, "Your idea. You do it."

Holly shook her head. "He already knows you don't know who he is. You take the picture. I'll use Kari's computer to do the image search. If he's someone famous, I can go in and pretend I recognize him. He might need the flattery. "

Marley made a face. "Darn it, that makes sense. Wait, you already saw him when you served him."

"Sure, and of course I recognized him right away, but I was too shy to say anything. I finally got up my nerve to ask for his autograph."

Holly sounded so sincere that Marley might have believed her if she hadn't already known the truth. Marley would never be able to pull that off. Sneaking a picture might be the easier chore after all.

A text came from Adam: Looks like I'm fostering five kittens. Send help.

Marley smiled. Poor Adam. Well, if he could take care of the kittens, she could get some guy's picture. She sent him a kiss emoji.

Marley looked up at Holly. "All right, I'm going to do this." She tugged the tails of her button-up shirt to straighten it. "Agent Marley reporting for duty. Wait, how do I do this? I need coffee first." She leaned over the table, took a sip of coffee, and ate her hard-boiled egg in three bites. One needed energy for secret missions.

"Walk in there with your phone out," Holly said. "Take pictures of cats. If anyone asks, you're getting some shots for social media. We really will post some photos, so they'll be there if someone checks. Get this guy in a few of them."

"How close do I have to get?"

"Really close." Holly leaned toward her, stopping only six inches away from Marley's face. "This close."

When Marley drew back, eyes wide, Holly laughed. "Kidding. Not that close. Ten feet should work. We can always zoom in on the photo. Try to get one with him facing you, and maybe one in profile as well."

"Okay. Fine." Marley ran through the scenario in her mind as she quickly ate her yogurt. She took a last gulp of coffee. It felt wrong to leave her trash on the table, especially with the yogurt splatter, but she needed to get moving. He might finish his "adequate" snack and leave.

Plus, if she didn't go now, she might lose her nerve.

She pulled out her phone and opened the photo app. She nodded at Holly.

The barista saluted. "Godspeed, agent Stevens."

Marley gave a weak chuckle and headed for the big room.

The guy was down to the last two samples. Good thing he ate slowly, maybe because he was scribbling in a notebook. What could he be writing? Would that give them a clue?

She took a picture of Autumn curled in a cat hammock. As she passed behind the possible British actor, she peeked over his shoulder, but his handwriting was illegible. Maybe he was a doctor rather than an actor.

Marley stopped by the older couple playing with Salt and Pepper. "Do you mind if I get a picture for our social media feed?" She pitched her voice to carry to the other guy. "It's good publicity for the café and helps the cats get adopted."

"Oh, of course." The woman smiled. "I love these two, but my husband says we have enough pets at home." She touched her hair. "What do I need to do?"

"Just keep playing. Salt and Pepper seem delighted with your attention." She snapped a few photos while the woman swung the feathered fishing line enthusiastically. Marley ought to be taking video. None of these photos would come out sharp. Oh well, that was not their priority at the

27

moment. Anyway, cats blurred in motion sometimes made great pictures.

She glanced over at the mysterious man. He was watching her. Was that good or bad? Hopefully he heard her excuse for taking pictures, but she could hardly turn the camera on him while he paid such close attention. Unless she dared ask him directly for a photo?

No, that might mess up Holly's plan for later.

"Thank you, these are great." She moved away from the older couple and took a few other random pictures of cats. Merlin, the Maine Coon, perched on a chair with his head up and his paws crossed in front of him, regal as a sphinx. That would make an excellent social media post. They always got people coming in asking about a specific cat if they posted a truly wonderful photo.

Even better, after Marley crouched to take a few close-ups of Merlin on the chair, she rose slightly and got a shot of the man almost face on.

Should she zoom in now, or take more distant photos and let Holly crop them on the computer? Marley knew those decisions made a difference in photo quality, but she wasn't sure how. She tried both.

The man sipped his cappuccino and picked up his next-to-last bakery treat. Marley needed to get the profile photo ASAP.

He was about fifteen feet from the back room that held the litter boxes, which was to his right side. She'd been planning to scoop anyway. She moved to the door and paused with her hand on the handle. She turned slightly sideways and glanced back.

The man lifted his cappuccino to his lips.

Marley opened the door, turning with it and lifting her phone. As he put down the cup, she tapped the screen a couple of times.

His gaze shifted toward her. She jerked her arm down.

The phone almost dropped from her fingers. She clutched it and stared at the screen, randomly tapping it with her thumb as if sending a message. She'd have a few photos of the floor. So what?

She ducked into the back room without looking up and closed the door behind her. Three cats slept in the cat beds back there. They could enter through the pet flap, giving them privacy if they didn't feel sociable.

Holly still had to do the image matching thing and get back in there to talk to him if he turned out to be anyone interesting. If he was famous, but he left before they finished, they'd have done nothing except figure out what opportunity they'd missed.

She had the barista's number, since they sometimes needed to communicate for scheduling. She could e-mail the pictures, but she'd need time to find the best pictures and send them.

Marley quickly scooped the biggest chunks from the fullest litter boxes. Her watch buzzed with a text coming in. Maybe Holly had a message for her. Marley used the back of her thumb to bring up the text.

Adam again: Bring Brian to my place after school.

Marley frowned. Of course Brian would love to see the kittens, but maybe she shouldn't let him. He'd only get attached and be upset when he couldn't keep them.

She ignored the text and washed her hands. Adam could wait. Her current mission couldn't.

She crossed the big room without glancing at the rude man. Was he watching her? Did she really feel his gaze, or was it merely her nerves?

She slipped through the door and ran the few steps down the hallway to the kitchen door. She barreled through.

Holly jumped back out of the way. "Stand down, agent."

Marley jerked back with a gasp. "Sorry." The kitchen door swung both ways to make it easy for servers to go through with full hands. They were supposed to do that slowly so as not to bump anyone. She'd forgotten.

"Did you get the pictures?"

Marley pulled out her phone. "I wasn't sure if I should e-mail them to you or what."

Holly plucked the phone from her hand. "You have the same phone as Kari, right? She keeps a charging cable in her office. I'll connect this to her computer. Do I need a password?"

"Oh, right." Marley turned and pushed the door open, more gently this time. A couple had paused inside the entrance to look through the interior windows at the cats. "We'll be right with you," Marley called.

She hurried down the hall to Kari's office, glancing back as she unlocked it. If they really wanted to, the visitors could snatch something from the counter and flee before she returned, but that seemed unlikely.

She led the way into the office. Fortunately, she'd left the computer on after getting the info on the vet for Adam. She only needed to input the password.

She left Holly there. Would Kari mind? Normally baristas didn't get on the company computer. But this was a special case.

She stopped outside the door and took a deep breath. If only Kari were there. Kari always knew what to do and how to do it, or at least she acted with so much confidence that you believed she did. Marley appreciated having the responsibility for the opening shift, because it showed her sister's trust. It also meant Marley had to run everything herself for hours. Why did people assume she could handle these things?

The couple stood by the counter, examining the specials board. Marley pulled her hair into a ponytail as she hurried back to the kitchen. She grabbed her apron and smiled at the couple. "May I help you?"

She took their order and made their drinks. Then she finally cleaned up her splattered yogurt. After that, she checked the items in the display case and restocked anything running low. They'd be hitting the lunch rush soon.

Another text came through from Adam. It had a photo attached, but she couldn't see it on her watch, and Holly had her phone.

Where was Holly? Marley leaned over the counter to check on the man.

He was standing. Was he going to play with cats? Was he leaving?

He turned slowly in a circle, as if studying the room. Marley jerked out of sight as his circle aimed him toward her

Should she get Holly? Try to delay the guy if he left?

She leaned forward. The door to the big room swung open. The man stepped through.

Marley couldn't think of anything to say to get him to stop.

He glanced in her direction. She managed a weak smile and said, "Thank you. Come again soon."

He nodded once and headed away down the hall.

Marley leaned her elbows on the counter, put her head in her hands, and groaned. All that work for nothing.

Holly came back a minute later. She had a strange expression as she handed Marley her phone. "You got a text or something."

Marley checked it. "Oh, Adam sent photos of the kittens. Aren't they sweet." Too sweet. Sweet enough to break a nine-year-old boy's heart. She couldn't take Brian to see them.

She texted back: Not a good idea.

Marley tossed her head. "I'm afraid the guy left. I couldn't think of how to keep him any longer."

Holly sat at the table. "That's okay. I don't think we want to ask for his autograph."

31

"Oh? Why, is he someone horrible? Or couldn't you find him at all?"

Another text came from Adam: Trust me.

"I found him." Holly bit her lip for a second. "He's the restaurant reviewer for the local paper."

"Oh? Ah." Marley slumped against the counter. "That's … adequate."

Chapter 5

Adam paced his apartment. He flipped through a computer magazine but none of the articles caught his attention. He stopped at the window and stared out without seeing anything.

He hoped he wasn't making a huge mistake. He didn't think so, but it was a lot of responsibility. He'd gotten his rhythm at his new job, but it still got intense at times. The first few months, he'd been in California for training. Now he should be staying home, with normal hours.

Except "normal" didn't always mean 40 hours at a place like that. He rarely left work before six, and often not until seven. No one said he had to stay that late, but he wanted to make a good impression.

He imagined telling his boss, his coworkers, that he had to leave at five every day to feed kittens. People with human children didn't use that excuse to leave early.

To take care of the kittens, he'd have to establish boundaries and keep them, with himself as much as with anyone else. But if he didn't want to work 60, 70-hour weeks, he should establish that now. They wanted his skills. He'd give the job everything he had for 40 hours a week. If they couldn't pull off the project with that amount of his time, that was management's fault. They needed to hire more people.

He nodded to himself. But he knew it wouldn't be that easy.

A knock came at the door. He hurried to open it.

Marley smiled but she looked worried. Brian glared around the room. He'd refused to go to the café since his favorite kitten had been adopted. Maybe Kari and Marley had made a mistake thinking the café would fill the boy's need for a pet companion. He loved deeply and mourned equally. No wonder Brian looked so suspicious now.

Adam waved them into the room. "Come meet the kittens."

Brian's gaze locked on the box sitting on the coffee table, echoing with mews. And yet he hung back in the doorway, looking like someone was dragging him to be tortured.

"Don't you want to see them?" Marley asked softly.

He took a step in. "Not if I can't have them." And yet he took another step.

Adam caught Marley's anguished look from the corner of his eye, but he didn't glance at her. She was ready to bolt with the boy.

Adam had to make this work. "They need to be fed by bottle every two hours. The vet showed me how. And there's other stuff." He leaned toward Brian and whispered, "You have to help them pee and poop."

Brian giggled.

"Every two hours?" Marley looked from the box to Adam. "You can't do that, not with your job."

Brian crept close enough to see over the edge of the box. "Who's going to do that stuff?"

He took another step and knelt by the box. "I could help if they were at the café." His hand curled around the black kitten. Good, he'd been hooked by the little bundles of cuteness. "Mom said we couldn't take them there."

"The vet agreed," Adam said. "For one thing, they need to be fed at night too. Someone would have to stay at the café overnight."

Brian looked interested at that, but Marley said, "Forget it, Bud. Remember, we talked about the health issues as well. And these guys are too young to be with the older cats."

"There's too much going on at the café," Adam said. "Customers going in and out, the cats playing and sometimes

34

fighting. That's not the best environment for these little guys. When they're older, when they've been fixed and had all their vaccinations, then they'll be ready for adoption."

Brian had both hands in the box, letting the kittens squirm against him. "So that's it? We just have to send them away?"

"No. I had an idea. I thought we could raise them." Adam looked at Marley. "The three of us."

Brian hunched over the box, his hair hiding his face. "We can't have them at our house because Grandma's allergic."

"No, but I can keep them at my house. The thing is, I can't stay home with them all the time. We'll have to take turns. I'll give them bottles overnight. You and your mom can come by after school, and in the evenings if you want."

Brian's eyes shone, but Marley said, "Adam, that's sweet, but to run back and forth from our house to here, it took twenty minutes and it will be worse going home. With the feeding, that's over an hour each time."

"As to that, I've signed the paperwork to buy a house. It's empty, so I think they'll be happy to have me move in as soon as possible. It'll be a while before it's furnished, but that shouldn't matter to the kittens."

Marley's eyebrows went up. "And where is this house?"

He shoved his hands in his pockets and shuffled his feet. "About a block and a half away from yours."

"Adam! You're moving back to our neighborhood?" She smiled, and his shoulders dropped.

"Yeah. I missed it too much. I missed all of you too much." Before she could read too much into that, he added, "I got a good deal on the house."

"How can you afford to buy something at your age?"

His shoulders hunched back up. "I'm not that young. I got a signing bonus from my company. I have a good salary. The bank was happy to work with me on the mortgage."

She reached out to touch his arm. "Adam, I'm sorry. I didn't mean to be insulting. It's just crazy to think of you already buying a house, when it's still a distant dream for me."

"Home is a good dream," he said. For a moment, the room seemed to hold only the two of them. "You'll get your house someday."

He wished it could be his house. That was one reason he'd chosen that neighborhood, even though his own mother had moved away. He knew Marley wouldn't want to be far from her mother. Kari was already talking about moving in with Colin. They wouldn't want to abandon Diane entirely, not when she still mourned her husband. Besides, Diane helped take care of Brian, and no one turned down free babysitting.

His dream was silly, to think that he and Marley and Brian might share a house someday. Maybe the best dreams were foolish.

Brian was talking. Adam and Marley had held each other's gazes for a long time, maybe longer than ever before.

She broke away.

Could she have felt what he felt? The pounding of the heart, the damp palms? Had they really shared that kind of moment? Or was her smile merely gratitude that he was including Brian in the kitten project?

Adam shook away his thoughts and turned his focus to the boy. "I'm sorry, what was that?"

"I can come by before school too."

"If your mom and grandma say it's okay. We'll have to find someone to take shifts when I'm at work and you're at school. Maybe Kari and Colin can split it. Or maybe your grandma can stop by on her lunch hour. She manages all right for a few minutes. Well, it takes over half an hour to give them all food, but I think she could handle that once a day."

36

"When they're older, we have to give them up, right?" Brian looked desperately anxious for the answer.

"Well … I don't think I can keep five cats."

Brian's face fell.

"But I wouldn't mind keeping one."

Brian's smile exploded. "How about two? So they can be friends."

Adam laughed. "Friends are good. Maybe two."

"How about –"

"Don't push it," Marley said. "We'll help raise these guys. When they're old enough, Adam can choose the *one* – or possibly two, if he decides on that – he wants to keep and you can still visit them."

Brian nodded and looked into the box. Adam could read his expression. How could anyone give up any one of these kittens?

Adam sat cross-legged beside Brian and peered into the box. "Your mom isn't quite right. We will raise them, and then you choose the one." He glanced up at Brian's gaze. "Maybe two, that you want to keep. They'll have to live at my house, at least for now, but they'll be your cats. You can visit them whenever you want, as often as you want."

Adam glanced up at Marley. "When your mom says it's okay, of course."

Brian twisted to throw his arms around Adam and hugged tightly. "Thank you."

Adam hugged him back and grinned at Marley.

She bit her lip, her eyes moist. She met his gaze and whispered, "Thank you" as well.

Chapter 6

On Saturday morning, Marley headed to Adam's new house as soon as she finished her shift at the café. She didn't normally work on Saturdays, but she'd traded with Colin so he could help Adam. Since she got to bake, and Colin had to do manual labor, she felt she'd gotten the best of the deal.

The front door stood open. Male laughter carried from somewhere in the house.

Marley called out as she entered. "Hello! Cupcake delivery." She looked for a place to leave her purse. A bed sat in the middle of the otherwise-empty living room. It had a rumpled, dark blue cover and a surprising number of pillows. Why did a single guy need a king-sized bed?

Adam was quite tall. Probably he hung off the end of most beds.

Anyway, tossing her purse on his bed felt too intimate. Marley looped the strap over the inside handle of the front door.

After some thumps and thuds, grinning men emerged from the hallway into the living room.

Goodness, that was a lot of testosterone. Adam, tall and lean. Colin, fit in his black T-shirt with the tattoo peeking out one sleeve. Jamar, with his eyes the color of chocolate syrup and his smile bright against his dark skin. Luis, the smallest of the bunch, but with a big swagger and an easy, flirtatious manner. And all of them streaked with plaster dust. She might start ovulating simply being in the same room.

"Just what we needed," Luis said. "A beautiful woman to ease our suffering."

"Hello, gorgeous!" Jamar grinned. "Let me take those for you."

"So chivalrous." She passed over the box. "Those are chocolate cherry cupcakes and Boston cream cupcakes. If someone doesn't like chocolate, they're out of luck."

Jamar winked. "If someone doesn't like chocolate, they're crazy."

Adam squeezed between the two of them. "You can take those into the kitchen. Marley, do you want a tour? Most of the house doesn't look like much yet, but we're getting the bedroom fixed up this weekend."

"That will be nice for you." She didn't care about construction, but she followed him down the hall to be polite. Okay, and also because exploring other people's houses was delightfully nosy.

He paused in the hallway, with open doors on either side. "Four bedrooms, two baths."

Four bedrooms? He'd bought a lot of house, surely far more than he needed, unless he was planning to rent to roommates.

"The previous owners lived here for over thirty years, and I don't think they did any updates in that time."

She murmured an agreement. No wonder he got a good deal. Not only did everything look worn, but the previous owners apparently liked flowers. Flowered wallpaper. Long floral curtains that hung down past regular windows, reaching to the floor. Even the carpet had a splotchy pattern reminiscent of flowers.

He stopped at the last room and gestured through the door. She peered in from the hallway. They'd pulled up the carpet and stripped the walls. A window-shaped hole showed some trees in the backyard.

"Come to think of it," Adam said, "this doesn't look like much yet either. But it's such a relief to have all that flowered stuff out of here. We're putting in a bigger window, double-paned. That was Colin's idea. I hadn't even thought of changes like that."

39

He gave a sheepish grin and shrugged. "Probably because I had no idea how to do stuff like that. We'll paint the walls, I think the color is called eggshell, and put in this flooring."

He turned and pointed to the room across the hall. Stacks of what looked like smooth wood boards filled the room. "You just snap the pieces together. Fairly cheap, and environmentally friendly. It's made of bamboo."

"It's going to be like a whole new house." Marley smiled at him encouragingly.

"It'll take months to get the whole thing done." He shoved his hands in his pockets and his shoulders hunched up. "I can't expect Colin and his buddies to spend every weekend here. But I'm learning how to do some of this stuff, so I can work on it myself a room at a time."

"In between feeding kittens? I assume Brian is with them."

"Yeah, he's taken every feeding since eight o'clock this morning. No surprise that he's more interested in kittens than construction. They're in the kitchen." They headed back that way.

"You managed to take care of them yourself yesterday?"

"I took them to work." Adam chuckled. "I think everybody in the company stopped by. I even got help with the feedings. I'm not claiming I got a lot of work done, but I could probably find homes for all the kittens if I wanted."

Marley stopped him with a touch to his arm. "You won't?"

He turned and gazed down at her. In the narrow hallway, their faces were only a foot apart. "I won't. I promised Brian he could keep one." He leaned closer and his breath brushed past her ear as he whispered, "I'm already planning to keep two for sure, but I'll let him think he's talking me into that."

"Good plan." Marley fought the urge to rub at the tingle that ran over her ear and down her neck. "Otherwise he'd talk you into all five by the end of the month."

"It's going to be hard to give up any of them as is." He moved away, and she followed, glad for the extra space.

They entered the kitchen, and Marley's gaze flew to Brian. She hadn't seen him since she peeked in on him in bed that morning, before she headed to the café. He looked fine, content and sweet with one hand holding a bottle and the other tucked around a kitten.

She glanced around the kitchen. Yep, floral linoleum, and wallpaper with big flowers, orange no less. The house needed a lot of work. Too bad Adam couldn't stay in his apartment full-time while it got done, as he'd planned. Still, it was nicer to have the kittens here.

Marley crossed to the counter that had been set up with kitten feeding and cleaning supplies. "Did you get a cupcake?"

"When I'm done. I have one more kitten to go." Brian put down the bottle. He grabbed a soft paper towel and dipped it in a mug of water.

"Wash your hands before you eat."

"Mom, I know."

Marley glanced into the cupcake box on another counter. Would a dozen cupcakes be enough for four active men, and one small boy? It had seemed like a lot when she packed them. Not so much now, with six already gone. She resisted the urge to take one herself. She'd already had a muffin *and* a scone that morning.

"Coffee, tea, water?" Adam asked.

"I'm glad to see you have the important things set up. Whatever is easiest."

"I'll make another pot of coffee anyway. The fridge is stocked with sodas as well, but coffee goes better with cupcakes." He crossed to a coffee pot set up at the end of

41

that counter. The orange wallpaper made the kitchen seem small, but it was actually quite spacious.

"Let me. You've been working."

He gave her a crooked smile. "And you haven't?"

"Well, not physical labor. Okay, kind of physical, but not pulling up carpet and stripping wallpaper." Her feet and legs did ache though. One of the three chairs had been left open, no doubt for her. She'd feel guilty taking it.

Adam touched her shoulder. "Have a seat. Let someone wait on you for a change."

Fine. These guys were polite, and they were setting a good example for Brian. Colin had one of the chairs, maybe in deference to the prosthesis that replaced his lower leg. Jamar leaned against the wall.

Luis patted the empty chair next to him. "Come on, don't be shy."

She sat.

Colin licked his fingers. Marley wanted to ask if he'd washed his hands after handling all the dirty construction stuff. Sometimes it was hard to repress the mothering instinct.

"Fantastic," Colin said. "Pretty, too."

"I can't take credit for that," Marley said. "I don't know if we got lucky, or if Kari knew she was hiring two baristas with artistic skills. Dustin did these. He's a bit better with frosting, but Holly has the edge with foamed milk designs. I don't know how many times her cappuccino art has been on Instagram."

"They're both talented," Colin said. "Speaking of talent, I noticed a flyer for a singing contest."

"Oh. That." She'd carefully avoided looking at it since that first time.

Colin looked up at the ceiling. "Now let me see … who have I heard sing?"

Marley shifted uncomfortably. She wished she hadn't taken the seat at the table, surrounded by all of them. She'd be more comfortable over in the kitchen, puttering around, where she could duck out of sight behind a cabinet.

"You sing?" Jamar asked. "Cool. You should totally do that contest."

Adam put a cup of coffee beside her. With milk, the way she liked it.

She took a sip to delay. Cleared her throat. Tried to look casual and indifferent. "Nah. Who has time?"

"Kari would say you make time for the things you love," Colin said.

Marley's sister had been saying that lately. It was totally annoying. Kari was supposed to find more time for the things *she* loved, not nag Marley to do the same.

Marley shrugged. "I don't trust it anyway. It's probably some moneymaking scam."

"No way, man," Jamar said. "We go to that bar all the time." He glanced at Brian. "Well, not daily or anything, but once in a while. The owner's cool. Me and my boys play there sometimes."

"Your boys?" Marley asked. "Oh, you mean like a band?"

"Jazz trio, nothing fancy. I play the upright bass." Jamar made finger motions as if strumming a cello. "We're not pros. We get together every week to jam, play in public once in a while for fun."

"Upright bass is one of my favorites," Marley said. "That deep sound is so sexy."

Jamar bowed. "That's me, so sexy."

Luis snorted. "So screwy, more like."

Jamar pushed off the wall and got Luis in a headlock. The guys wrestled and bantered playfully.

Marley laughed. Brian watched everything as he fed the last kitten. It was good for him to spend time around men.

43

He hadn't had much male influence since his grandfather died over a year before. Well, except for Adam. But he was a certain type of guy, more geeky than manly.

Marley winced at her own thoughts. She had a nine-year-old son who'd rather feed kittens than play with his friends. She adored how sweet and sensitive Brian was. She tried to raise him to see females as equal to males. "Girly" should never be an insult. How could she think macho men were a better influence on him? Maybe she had some work to do on her own internal stereotypes.

She rose and went to her son. "How's it going?" She slid an arm around him. "Aw, what a little cutie. Do they have names yet?"

"No. I've been thinking about it."

"They need names."

"Yeah, but Mom, you should do that singing thing."

Marley drew back to see his face better. "Really? You want me to try a singing contest? It would mean being out in the evenings." That was their time together.

"Yeah, but you're really good. Grandma said you wanted to be a singer when you were a kid."

"Grandma said that, did she?" Boy, Marley's whole family was determined to annoy her today. "I did, but it was only …" She couldn't dismiss a childhood dream, not to Brian. She wanted to encourage him to dream big and believe he might achieve anything. Life would teach him otherwise soon enough.

She finally said, "I like singing as a hobby, that's all. I only do it for fun."

"The contest will be fun," Jamar said. "We'll come cheer you on."

Great, they were all listening in on her conversation. And they weren't going to let her off with easy excuses.

She could simply say no, and call it final. 'Because I said so' was a perfectly good reason if you were a mom. No one could make her do the contest.

So why was she hesitating?

Because she wanted to show Brian that she still had dreams and would work to follow them?

Because part of her regretted not pursuing a singing career?

Because deep down, she wondered if she could do it?

The kitten made a last few halfhearted licks at the formula. Brian put down the bottle and reached for a paper towel.

"Here, I'll do that," Marley said. "You wash up and get your cupcake."

Brian handed over the kitten with clear reluctance. "Okay, but what about the singing contest?"

Marley's heart pounded. Her head felt hot.

She held the kitten over a wad of paper towels, dipped a clean towel in the mug of warm water, and started dabbing at the kitten to clean it. Dealing with pee and poop. That she could handle.

But could she do more?

Brian was waiting. Everyone was waiting.

"I'll think about it, okay?

Brian nodded and took a chocolate cherry cupcake from the box. He sat in her abandoned chair and began eating.

Marley peeked in the box. "Anyone else need one?"

Jamar patted his stomach. "I've had one of each already."

"I guess I'm behind." Adam took a Boston cream cupcake and ate it leaning against the counter.

Luis refilled his coffee, giving Marley a wink as he passed by. She finished cleaning up the kitten and put it back in the box with the others.

Colin stood. "We should get back to work if we want to finish the room this weekend."

Adam put down his coffee mug and pushed away from the counter.

Brian looked up. "We were going to name the kittens."

Adam looked at Brian and then the other men. He turned back to Brian. "Go ahead and name them. You can tell me later."

Colin clapped Adam on the shoulder. "You stay here. The window goes in next. We don't need four guys for that."

"You mean you don't need me getting in the way while you do the work," Adam said. "Fine. You go be useful, and I'll name kittens."

The rest of the men filed out. "Tell us when we can hear you sing," Jamar said.

Brian dropped the cupcake paper in a garbage can set against the wall and crossed to the kitchen. He washed his hands and leaned over the kitten box. "Naming kittens is useful," he said softly. "They need names."

Adam stood beside him. "You're right, they do. We need to be able to talk about them. We need their names when we post adorable pictures online. It wouldn't do to say, 'Kittens numbers one, two, three, four, and five.'"

Brian smiled as he looked down at the kittens. Was his obsession with them a good or bad thing? Marley couldn't tell.

She started to close the cupcake box. "Brian, you only had one. Do you want one of the other kind?"

Brian glanced at the box. "Is that the one with goop in it?"

"It's vanilla pudding in between the cupcake layers. You like vanilla pudding."

Brian turned back to the kittens. "I like pudding by itself, not in cupcakes."

Marley shook her head. "Fine, I'm not going to pressure you to eat cupcakes." She was probably a terrible mother as it was, giving him sweets. But she didn't want to prohibit them and make them seem even more special. Plus, it would be hypocritical, given that she was a baker and ate plenty of sweets herself.

Parenting was tough.

Adam leaned on the counter opposite her. "Are you really going to think about the singing contest?"

That again. "Do you think I should?" Why did she care what he thought anyway? It was her decision, no one else's.

For a while Adam simply looked at her. She liked that about him, he didn't rush to answer, like he knew what was best. He thought about things. Maybe that's why she wanted to hear his opinion.

"It's up to you, of course," he said at last. "I love hearing you sing. We all do. If you do it, we'll cheer you on, no matter what happens. Maybe you don't want strangers judging you. I get that."

"It's scary," she admitted.

Brian glanced over at her. "You always tell me I should try things that are scary."

"Oh, and *now* you listen to me? Don't you have kittens to name?" She wanted to scream that she was almost 30. She shouldn't have to do scary things anymore! Her life should already be the way she wanted it to be.

Yeah, right.

Marley blew out a breath. "Fine, I'll look into it."

She caught a flash of Brian's grin before he hid his smile by looking down at the kittens. At least she'd be setting a good example.

Adam reached across the counter to touch her elbow. Marley turned her attention to him.

47

"You should do what makes you happy." He looked deep into her eyes. "No matter what happens, we'll know you're perfect."

Perfect. Ha. She couldn't even see perfect from where she stood. But she didn't mind having one person who saw her that way.

Chapter 7

Adam ought to feel guilty about letting the other guys work on his house without him. He could at least stand by, ready to hand them tools or bring them cold drinks. Besides, he was trying to learn some skills so he could work on the house by himself later.

But hanging out with sweaty guys in a crowded, dusty room, or out here with Marley and Brian? No contest.

He liked seeing Marley in his kitchen. He'd like it more if the surroundings weren't quite so orange, but he had plans for that. They included asking Marley for lots of advice on remodeling a kitchen. That was one sure way to get her interested in spending time with him.

Not to mention, should he ever persuade her to move in, she'd have the kitchen of her dreams.

Marley touched the kitten that had orange and white swirls. "Curled up like this, he looks like a cinnamon bun."

"Mom, that one's a girl."

"Fine, she looks like a cinnamon bun."

"That's a good name," Adam said. "Cinnamon Bun."

They looked at him. Did they think it was stupid?

"Come on," he said, "Cinnamon Bun is a cute name for a cat, especially one that turned up at a bakery." He nudged Brian. "But it's up to you."

Brian gently scooped up the kitten in both hands and held it six inches from his face. "Cinnamon Bun." His brows drew together as he studied the sleepy little face. "She likes it."

"Excellent," Marley said. "I'll be able to remember this one and recognize her from her pattern. One down, four to go. Should we keep the bakery theme? We could call them, let's see … Brownie, Lemon Bar, Scone, Muffin?"

Brian scrunched up his nose. "Not Muffin."

Marley propped one hand on her hip. "Oh, you're okay with Lemon Bar and Scone, but you draw the line at Muffin?"

Brian giggled. "I didn't say the other names were okay." He put Cinnamon Bun back in the box and studied the other kittens. "Maybe Brownie for this one." He picked up the black kitten and gave it the same close scrutiny. "Yes, Brownie."

Adam touched a kitten that was mostly black but with a white patch on the back, kind of like a saddle. He might have suggested an equestrian name, but the baked goods theme worked. "This one looks like a chocolate cupcake with white frosting. How about Cupcake?"

Over the next few minutes, they settled on Cupcake, along with Sugar Cookie (Sugar for short) for the white kitten with specks of tan, and Peanut Butter Cookie (Cookie for short) for the one with a light brown pattern.

"Okay." Marley blew out a breath and pushed the curls off her forehead. "We have Cinnamon Bun, Brownie, Cupcake, Cookie, and Sugar." She touched each of the kittens in turn. "I might forget and you'll have to remind me, okay? I might accidentally call them Rocky Road and Banana Nut and Croissant. And of course, Muffin."

Brian snickered. "It's only five kittens, Mom."

Marley shook her head. "You don't know how full my brain is. Do you want to head home now, or is that a stupid question?"

Brian shook his head. "I'll stay here."

"You have a while before the next feeding. Did you bring a book or anything?"

"No. It's okay."

Adam picked up the box. "Let's move this to the table. You can sit down and hold the kittens on your lap."

"One at a time," Marley said.

"Unplug the heating pad and grab the cord," Adam said.

They maneuvered the box into its new spot. Brian settled down with Sugar on his lap. That was funny, sugar on his lap. They were going to get some weird statements using these names.

"I guess I'll go," Marley said. "If you don't need me."

She was talking to Brian, of course, but Adam wanted to answer. He said merely, "I'll walk you out."

He paused in the living room. He hadn't made his bed. Would she think he was a slob?

Never mind. Don't think of the bed.

He turned away from it. "I was thinking we should take Brian along whenever we take the kittens to the vet for vaccinations or whatever. He seems really interested in their care."

"You think he might want to become a vet? I know he loves animals, but he's not great with math. Don't veterinarians have to know a lot of math, like doctors?"

Adam shrugged. "I'm sure it involves a lot of science, but I don't know how often vets have to do mathematical computations. They probably have programs to do the math, or at least lists that tell them how much medicine for the weight of the patient and so forth. Wouldn't you think?"

"I have honestly never thought about it, but I guess so."

Adam thought of Jenna. "Brian could ask the vet about that. She's pretty brusque, but I think she'd be willing to talk to a kid like Brian who so clearly loves animals. If not her, maybe one of the vet techs. I was in the back room while they worked. It was interesting."

"Brian would love that, as long as there aren't any animals dying while he's there."

"We'll check before we take him in."

"Thanks." Marley put her hand on Adam's upper arm and squeezed. "You're a good friend." She frowned at his

51

arm and squeezed again. "You have some muscles there, Mister. When did that happen?"

He gave a little snort. Man, why did he have to sound like a twelve-year-old when he laughed?

"I keep active," he said. "Now Colin has me trying power yoga."

"You guys are getting pretty close. I wasn't sure when you first met. You seemed …" Marley trailed off.

"Yeah. I think it was because he liked Kari and wasn't sure if I was a threat." And Adam hadn't been sure if Colin was a rival for Marley. But he couldn't tell her that part. "Once Colin knew we weren't a couple, he and I have been okay."

"That's good." Marley looked at his chest. She shook her head with a little smile. "I can't stand it anymore."

She reached for the top button of his shirt. Adam's whole body went tight. He stood like a statue as she undid the button.

"You were up feeding kittens all night," she said. "You must be exhausted."

He stared over the top of her head at the faded rose-patterned wallpaper across the room. Her fingers moved against his shirt. He didn't know what to do with his hands.

"I can see how you didn't notice." Her breath whispered against his throat. "But three other men in the house all morning, plus my son. None of them mentioned that you did your buttons up wrong?"

Her hands moved down his chest. She undid one button and then fixed it through the proper hole. She never exposed more than an inch or so of his skin. But her warm breath found that inch. The heat spread across his chest, down his limbs.

Her hands worked lower, over his stomach. His abs trembled as if he'd been doing a plank for two minutes. His fingernails dug into his palms.

She was fixing his buttons like she might do for her child. She didn't know the effect she had. He couldn't let her know.

But oh, it hurt.

Finally she tugged briskly on the loose tails of his shirt. "There," she said. "Much better."

He dropped his gaze to hers. Tried to smile.

Maybe she saw something in his face. She turned to look out the window. Adam closed his eyes and took two deep breaths before shifting to stand beside him her.

Marley gave him a sideways glance. "A lot of people expected you and Kari to get together at some point, but you never did." She stared out the window and added, "I wasn't sure if you even liked girls. Or boys. Or anyone."

Adam's face burned. He wanted to sink into the floor, disappear into the busy pattern of the carpet. Finally he spoke past the tightness in his chest. "I like girls. Women."

She glanced at him for a split second and turned away as her cheeks flushed pink. "It's none of my business. It's only, I never knew you to date anyone."

"Yeah, well." He shoved his hands in his pockets and shrugged. "I have gone on a few dates. Nothing serious." What the heck, he couldn't make things any worse. "They weren't the right person. I was in love with one particular girl. Woman. No one else measured up."

She swung toward him. "Kari?"

He huffed out a laugh. "No. Definitely not Kari."

She frowned, her forehead wrinkled, her skepticism clear. If she offered sympathy for her sister breaking his heart, he'd do something drastic.

He caught her gaze and held it. "Not Kari," he said firmly.

"Oh. I see. I … haven't dated much either. Not in a long time." She peered up at him with a nervous smile. "I guess we're two of a kind."

"Yeah. So." Was he going to do this?

He should do this. He might never get a better chance.

He might never get a worse chance, considering that she'd obviously never picked up on how he felt. But he wasn't getting anywhere by pining in silence. At least she'd wondered about his romantic life. That had to count for something, didn't it?

He looked out the window. "So … what would you think …" Yeah, coming on strong and confident there.

He turned toward her. Forced his shoulders down. Kept his gaze steady on her face even when she looked down at their feet.

"We could go on a date," he said. "You and I."

Her face lifted, eyes wide, mouth open.

He shrugged. "If you want. It might be fun."

Her mouth opened and closed a couple of times. "You mean like … for practice? Since we've done so little?"

"Sure, I guess." If that's what she had to call it to make it okay. He simply wanted a chance, however he could get one.

She turned away, toward the door.

"It's okay," he said. "You don't have to. I mean, of course you don't have to, you know that. I just mean … it's okay."

He was dying inside, but he couldn't bear to make her uncomfortable.

She peeked back over her shoulder. "I didn't say no. I'm thinking."

Thinking was good. Better than a no anyway. Anything was better than a no. He'd held this dream too long to give it up easily, but he wouldn't pester her if she turned him down.

Construction noises drifted from the back room, along with a faint rumble of voices. She'd probably rather go out with any of those guys. Well, not Colin, not her sister's boyfriend. But the other two. They didn't have any trouble flirting with her, letting her know they found her attractive and interesting.

A new sound came from the kitchen. Was that singing? Yes, Brian was singing a lullaby to the kittens. Adam couldn't make out the words, but the boy's voice was high and sweet. Adam had heard him sing along with Marley, but never alone.

At least everyone else was occupied. They wouldn't wander out here to see his humiliation.

Finally Marley twisted toward him. Adam resisted the urge to back away, to run, to avoid hearing her answer. He clenched his fists, forced his shoulders down, and looked into her face.

"Okay." She blew out a breath and touched her lips, as if she couldn't believe the words had come from her mouth. "Why not?"

"Okay. Good." His smile probably looked as uncomfortable as hers. But inside he was shouting for joy.

She picked up her purse and fiddled with the straps. "Don't tell anyone though, okay? I don't want Brian … or Kari … I don't want to tell anyone yet. You understand, right?"

He nodded. He wouldn't delve into her reasoning. He didn't need anyone to know either, in case he crashed and burned. If they kept this between the two of them, it would be easier to go back to 'just friends' if they failed.

Marley looked toward the kitchen. "I don't like to keep secrets. But some things …"

"Yeah," Adam said. "This is between the two of us. No one else needs to know."

"Okay. Well. Bye." She scurried out of the house. For once Adam was glad to see her go. He needed about an hour to over-think everything they'd said and stress about what to do next. He gave a longing glance at his bed, wanting to collapse on it.

Instead he headed for the back bedroom to help paint walls, hoping his smile didn't raise too many questions.

Chapter 8

Friday afternoon, Marley sat in the main café room with a decaf cappuccino, while two cats attempted to share her lap. Brian was feeding kittens in Kari's office. Keeping the kittens there during the day had been the simplest setup. Adam dropped them off on his way to work. Marley or Holly did a feeding after the morning rush. Kari and Colin took the next two feedings. Brian came to the café after school and did his homework in between two feedings. Adam picked up the kittens and took them to his house for the night. Brian usually got over there for at least one more feeding before his bedtime.

Her son seemed to have lost interest in everything else, but at least he was willingly going back to the café. He no longer seemed dragged down with the sadness he'd had since the kitten Shadow had been adopted. He'd even said a couple of school friends wanted to visit the kittens that weekend.

Someone passed by the windows that separated the hallway from the cat room. Was that Adam? The man had his lanky height and loose-limbed gait, but she didn't recognize the jacket or hat the man wore against the chilly drizzle.

As he placed his order, he pulled off the hat. Marley's heart gave a funny leap. It was Adam. She recognized him even at that distance, through the glare of the window, seeing only the back of his head and his shoulders.

They hadn't been alone together all week. She'd stopped by his house, but always with Brian, or to pick up Brian when he finished his kitten-care shift.

Adam sent her frequent photos of the kittens being adorable, and of Brian being adorable with the kittens. As if she didn't have enough of those on her phone.

She didn't, of course. She never could. And her mother insisted on seeing every one of them.

Adam's only reference to dating had been a short exchange way back on Sunday.

Busy next Saturday night?

No plans.

Plan to spend it with me. We'll have to take care of kittens.

Of course, the kittens couldn't be left alone for more than an hour or so. Adam couldn't ask someone else to watch the kittens, without raising questions. She'd thought dating was hard with a young child. This was going to be even more complicated.

Maybe it was just as well. Did she really want to date her little sister's best friend? Did she want to change the comfortable relationship she and Adam had always had?

He turned and smiled through the window, waving at her. Her heart gave that odd flip again.

Their relationship had already changed. They couldn't go back. Oh, they could go back to officially not dating. That was easy enough. If she said she'd changed her mind, he would accept it. But she couldn't go back to not knowing he wanted to date her. She'd never forget that. Things would be weird between them until they sorted it out one way or another.

They'd go on a date. Probably they wouldn't have any chemistry. They'd feel awkward, they'd laugh about it, they'd go back to being friends.

That was the best option. Wasn't it?

He slipped through the door into the main café, blocking Autumn as she tried to escape. Adam took off his jacket and gave it a shake. Autumn backed away with a hiss as water droplets scattered. It didn't deter Merlin, who trotted up

58

with a trilling mew. Adam crouched to greet the big Maine Coon. Merlin flopped on his side and let Adam rub him like one might a dog. Most cats didn't like that. Merlin did. Of course Adam had figured it out.

Marley did want someone in her life. She didn't meet many men. She saw plenty of new people at the café, but it wasn't a great place to get to know someone. A few times, someone had flirted with her across the counter, or when she went into the big room on her break. Either it ended there, and she never saw them again, or it ended when she brought up her nine-year-old son.

Adam stood and walked toward her. "Hey."

"Hey, yourself." Adam knew about Brian and loved him. Adam knew everything about Marley, and he still wanted to go on a date with her.

For practice, right? Simply so they could get a little more experience. She shouldn't take it too seriously.

She said, "Brian should be out any minute, and I'll have to force him through the tortures of homework."

He draped his jacket over a chair at the table next to Marley's. "I won't interrupt. I'm going to hang out here for an hour and then steal Kari away for dinner." Adam propped a satchel on the bench and pulled out a laptop. As he set it up on his table, a longhaired cat, white with beige and black patches, nosed at the satchel. That was either Ollie or Oscar – she could never keep those siblings straight.

Marley glanced at her watch. Brian should have finished feeding the kittens, though of course he would linger as long as possible, even though she'd warned him to come out as soon as he was done. She might have to go nag him. But her feet hurt, and the coffee tasted good. She'd give him a couple more minutes.

She yawned widely, caught Adam looking at her, and quickly covered her mouth. She gestured toward his computer. "It's after five on a Friday," she said. "Shouldn't you be done with work?"

"Oh, this isn't for my job."

She waited, but he didn't add anything. Did he want her to ask about it? Wouldn't he volunteer the information if he wanted her to know what he was doing?

A week ago, she simply would have asked. Now she felt shy. That was the problem with adding even the implication of romance to their friendship.

She should be normal. But nothing felt normal anymore.

The door swung open and her son came through. He grinned and waved. At her or at Adam, she couldn't tell.

He had to stop to pet every cat as he crossed the room. Marley tapped the small backpack sitting on the bench beside her. "Okay, Bud, get to work. Finish your homework now, and you'll have the weekend free."

He grabbed the bag, pulled out some papers, and slumped into the chair across from her. He shuffled the papers and studied them for about thirty seconds before turning to Adam. "What are you doing?"

Marley should probably get Brian back on track with his homework. But she really wanted to hear Adam's answer.

"Me? Nothing much. Writing a story."

"A *story* story?" Brian sat up straighter. "Like something to read for fun?"

"I hope so. It's fun for me anyway."

"What's it about?"

Adam glanced around the room. He leaned toward Brian and spoke in a low voice. "Bad men. Good men. Beautiful ladies. Fighting. Revenge. Lies. True love."

Marley lifted her coffee cup to hide her smile. That might not be an exact quote from *The Princess Bride*, but it was definitely a reference. How many times had they all watched that movie?

Brian's eyes widened. "All of that?"

"I hope so," Adam said. "Oh, and it's set in space. It's science fiction."

"Is it long?"

"I'm trying to write a whole novel. I'm about halfway finished, I think."

"It sounds good," Brian said.

Adam shrugged, glanced at Marley, looked away. "I don't know if it is. It doesn't matter. I'm having fun, and that's what counts."

Brian pushed at his homework. "Can I read it?"

"You can try, and tell me if it makes sense. Once you finish your homework. What are you working on?"

"Math." The word was a sigh of epic proportions.

"You don't make that sound like a good thing," Adam said.

"It's hard."

"Bring it over here. Maybe I can help."

Brian lost no time shuffling himself and his homework to Adam's table.

Dustin brought in Adam's order, a tall latte and a couple of their Chai Tea Shortbread Cookies. Marley's stomach grumbled, but it was almost time for dinner. Still, she didn't interrupt when Adam broke a cookie in half and gave part of it to Brian.

Adam and Brian got through the math homework in a lot less time, and with much less stress, than if Marley had been helping. She listened to make sure Adam wasn't doing the homework, but he simply led Brian through the problems and seemed to get her son to see the issues in a new light.

Maybe because he somehow worked cats into his examples. Why hadn't she thought of that?

No surprise Adam was good at math, since he was practically a genius at computers. More of a surprise that he was good at teaching math. In Marley's experience, people

61

who had a knack for something were often the worst teachers, since they didn't know how hard that thing was for other people. But maybe Brian had been picking up on her own dislike of math.

Adam seemed to make math fun for Brian, judging by their occasional snorts of laughter. Maybe they connected because Adam was so young.

No, she had to stop thinking of him that way. Adam was not a child. He was a full-grown man, with a good job and a new house. In many ways, he was more of a successful adult than she was.

Maybe she didn't like thinking of him as an adult because that led to thinking about adult things. Like kissing. If they dated, they'd probably kiss at some point.

She felt hot all over. She blew on her coffee, but that was not the source of the heat.

Brian put away his homework. Adam shifted the laptop closer to the edge of the table and tapped some keys. "Okay, here's the beginning of the story. Read as much as you want. Let me know if you have any ideas."

"Cool. I like writing. I'd like to write a story."

Really? That was the first Marley had heard of it. Maybe she got too caught up in the things he didn't want to do, because she had to push him to do them. She didn't spend as much time encouraging him to do the things he wanted to do. She knew he didn't have a problem with book reports, and he'd enjoyed writing the few little stories teachers had assigned. She'd never thought about it beyond her relief that she didn't have to nag him.

He still enjoyed their bedtime story ritual. Come to think of it, they'd gone from her making up stories for him, to him giving her ideas, to him telling almost as much of the story as she did. Funny how a child grew a tiny bit, day by day, until the change was huge and you didn't even notice it.

"I'm going to talk to your mom," Adam said. "It's hard watching someone read what you wrote."

Brian leaned over the laptop. Merlin hopped up beside him, and Brian put his arm around the big cat so they could both see the screen.

Adam moved to the chair across from Marley. "Oh, I had an idea," he said. "I'd like your advice on the kitchen. If you haven't already –" He glanced at Brian. "– made plans for tomorrow night, you could come over and help me."

"Sure, that works." She hadn't figured out what she was going to tell her mother, sister, and son to cover up their date. This was a perfect excuse. She'd tell them the truth about where she was going, and she'd be delighted to give him advice on that kitchen before they did … whatever else he had in mind.

She quickly changed the subject. "I didn't know you were a writer."

"I'm not, not really. I thought it would be fun to try a novel."

"Can I read it? Are you going to publish it?"

He squirmed like Brian trying to find a good excuse to avoid his chores. "I haven't really considered publishing. It probably isn't good enough."

"Wait a minute." Dim memories came back to her. "You wanted to be a writer once. You were writing stories … you must have been in middle school."

"Yeah. A long time ago." He pushed his hand through his hair, making it messier. "In high school, I did some fan fiction for TV shows I liked. Then I got busy with other stuff. I got the scholarship based on my math and science scores, and there's the whole making a living thing. Now I only write so I won't think about work all the time. Of course, with the kittens and the stuff I have to do in the house, I won't make much progress now."

"You should set aside some time for it. It's important to do things you enjoy, especially when you have so much else going on." Wait, where had she heard that advice lately?

He tipped his mug back to drain it, exposing the long line of his throat. Definitely not a child.

He set down the mug. "Like with you and singing?"

Hey, when did they switch to her? "I sing all the time. I don't have to enter some contest to do that."

"Does that mean you decided against it?"

Marley turned her empty cup around and around in her hands. "Actually, I did sign up. But I don't know. Do I really need the extra pressure? Maybe I should stick with singing for fun."

"Once you wanted to be a professional."

Her hands tightened on the cup. "That was a long time ago."

"Not that long. About the same time I was writing stories, as I recall. I'm not saying you made the wrong choice."

They both glanced at Brian. His attention seemed focused on the laptop and the cat.

"You made a very good choice," Adam said. "That doesn't mean you can't make new choices now. Don't you want to know?"

"Know what?" she whispered. "Either I find out I'm no good, or else I gave up that dream when I could have made it. What's the point? What am I going to do now, drag my son along on a world tour? Leave him behind?"

Adam leaned across the table, his voice as soft as hers. "I think you're jumping ahead of yourself. Does it have to be all or nothing? Some artists only perform locally, maybe put out an album or two."

He touched the back of her hand. She loosened her grip on the mug.

"You're so talented," he said. "If it were Brian, you would want him to use his gifts."

"Oh, like you're using your gift writing, but downplaying it, dismissing it?"

She shouldn't attack him. It wasn't fair. But she felt under attack, and she couldn't stop her defense.

Her words poured out. "You'll let a child read it, but I noticed you didn't answer when I asked to read it. You've never even mentioned your book to me before. Has Kari read it? Has anyone?"

"Hey, when did this become about me?" He gave a sheepish grin. "Okay, point taken. Maybe I shouldn't be so dismissive of my writing. But I don't know if I'm any good. We won't know until I finish it, if I ever do. We know you're a good singer."

This time his touch on her hand lingered. "Tomorrow night." His voice rumbled with promises. "We could do karaoke."

She raised her eyebrows. "And you'll sing too?"

He winced and returned to his normal voice. "I can if you want me to, but you've heard me sing before."

She chuckled. "I have. What about the kittens?"

"Oh, I'm sure they'd be better than I am, but we won't take them. I don't mind one gorgeous creature showing me up, but my ego balks at six of them."

She laughed. "Adam!"

"We start feeding them every three hours now. That gives us two hours to get to the bar, have a drink, sing, and get back. No problem."

It was only karaoke. If she was ever going to get up on stage, that was the easiest place to start. "I'll make you a deal. Karaoke tomorrow night. I'll sing. You won't." She leaned across the table and narrowed her eyes. "But you let me read your novel. Not someday. Now. As you write it."

65

His eyes widened and his throat moved as he swallowed. Was she asking too much? Maybe she should feel bad for putting him on the spot. But everyone seemed to think they were pressuring Marley for her own good. Why should she let him off the hook?

She couldn't promise to like his book. She could promise not to be mean if she didn't, but voicing that idea might make him more anxious.

"Okay," he said. "It's a deal."

Well, darn. Looked like she'd be singing in public the next night.

Chapter 9

Adam took a last look at himself in the bathroom mirror. They were going to a bar, not a fancy restaurant, so he wore jeans and a black button-up shirt. He'd gotten compliments when wearing that shirt. He splashed on a touch of cologne. Marley's and Kari's mother, Diane, had long since broken him of the teenage habit of overdoing the scent. He had to trust in his double application of deodorant to hide any sign of nerves.

He glanced at his watch. He could start feeding the kittens. He had intended to finish that before Marley arrived, but the new longer time between feedings had thrown off his schedule. Oh well, he wouldn't complain about spending more time with her, even in his ugly kitchen.

And it would give him something to do besides pace while he waited for her to arrive.

In the kitchen, he rolled back his sleeves and picked up Cupcake. The kittens were now big enough that they wanted to explore more. He let the black and white kitten totter around on the counter, blocking her when she reached the edges. The kittens might need fewer feedings, but they wanted more play time.

At least the bigger ones did. Cinnamon Bun and Cookie lagged behind the other three. They were a bit smaller. Runts? Weren't the runts of a litter often the ones who made the best pets later? He'd learned a lot about kittens in a short time, but every day reminded him of how little he still knew, and how much he only knew from cultural osmosis. He probably shouldn't count on those assumptions.

Finally he got Cupcake interested in the bottle. A knock came at the door. He yelled, "Come in!" At the sound of the front door opening, he added, "I'm in the kitchen."

Marley appeared in the kitchen doorway. She wore faded jeans and an oversized T-shirt, with her hair pulled back in a braid. She looked great, of course.

She didn't look like a woman excited about a date.

She gave him a tentative smile. "Hey."

Brian squeezed past her.

"I told him we didn't need help with the kittens," Marley said. "But, you know. I hope you don't mind."

"Never." Did this mean their date had become family time? At least Marley looked apologetic, so she probably hadn't planned things this way to force Adam to keep his distance.

Brian stopped across the counter from Adam and said, "Hi, Cupcake."

"Hi, Honey," Adam said. "Oh, you were talking to the kitten? Here, you can take over. We just started."

Brian slid his hands into place, and Adam released the kitten and the bottle.

Adam looked up at Marley – as Kari appeared beside her. He instantly felt guilty. He hadn't told his best friend that he was trying to go out with her sister. Had she figured it out? Had she come to put a stop to this date?

"I won't stay long," Kari said. "I want to see the new bedroom."

"Oh, sure." Adam rounded the counter to join the sisters.

Kari studied him. "You look nice. Going out tonight?"

He shuffled and squirmed, his face heating. "I thought I might, later."

She leaned closer and sniffed. "You smell nice too. Hot date?"

Kari was so short Adam could look right over her head. His gaze met Marley's in shared expressions of laughter and horror.

68

"Just … going to a bar," he said. "To listen to some music."

"Well, you look ready to impress the girls." Kari headed down the hallway.

Adam and Marley exchanged raised eyebrows and little shrugs as he slid past her to follow Kari.

Kari glanced into one of the untouched bedrooms and shuddered. "I still can't believe you bought this house of horrors, but Colin says it has great bones, whatever that means."

"It was big and cheap, and I like the location."

"Sure, Mom will drag you over for dinner all the time now." Kari got to the last bedroom and stopped in the doorway. "Wow."

Adam looked over her head. Did the room look as good as he thought, or had he been pummeled by the rest of the house so much that anything would look better?

The walls were now an inoffensive off-white color. The big window had double panes and a modern frame. He still hadn't made his bed – he was 100 percent sure he was not going to have company in it that night, so no need to impress – but the dark blue covers looked good against the light bamboo flooring.

Kari stepped into the room and turned in a slow circle. "If you do the whole place this well, you'll have an amazing home."

Yes. Not simply a house, but a home. Adam stood a little taller with pride, even though he'd had a lot of help with the labor. "It needs a few things on the walls, but I like it."

Kari rubbed the toe of one sneaker over the flooring. "The floor is pretty, but I expect carpet in a bedroom."

"I'm going to have two cats. I've already budgeted for one of those robot vacuums. Fun for them, and less work for me."

"Always thinking ahead."

Kari went back to the doorway, but she merely looked down the empty hallway. She grabbed Adam's arm and pulled him into the room.

Uh-oh. She'd figured out what Adam was doing with Marley, or at least trying to do. She was about to warn him off.

"You should take Marley out tonight."

"What?" He tried to keep his face innocent. He probably looked vacuous instead.

Kari stood close and whispered. "She doesn't go out enough. Left on her own, she'll watch a movie with Brian. You're going out anyway, so it's perfect. Drag her along. You can be each other's wingmen."

Adam tried to keep his laughter inside. "Okay, I'll try. If you think it's a good idea."

"Excellent." She tucked her arm through his and steered him toward the doorway. "I don't want to see her home before midnight."

"The kittens are due for a feeding at ten."

She paused halfway down the hallway. "That's too early." Kari glanced into the bathroom and winced. "I hope that's your next renovation."

"You don't like the pink toilet and tub? But they go so well with the pink tile on the walls, counter, and floor."

"So very much pink," Kari moaned.

"Actually, I was thinking the living room next, and then another bedroom for an office." And of course, the kitchen. But he wouldn't mention that to Kari. She knew Adam barely cooked when he was by himself. "The bathroom is outdated, but the plumbing works, and I don't spend much time in there."

"This is going to take forever. We need a plan to get it done quickly."

Of course, 'we' would. "I'm building a website for Jamar's jazz trio and doing some computer work for Luis' mother in trade for work time, so I'll have help."

"Good. I'll pitch in with project planning or whatever."

Adam chuckled to himself. Kari always had to have a plan, and once she got started, nothing would stop her. Love had softened his friend, but he was glad to see it hadn't completely changed her.

"Anyway, the kittens," she said. "I can take the ten o'clock feeding."

"You don't have plans with Colin?"

"Maybe I'll bring him along." She gave a smile he thought of as her 'Colin smile.' Adam had never seen it before Colin came into her life. Now it appeared a lot.

He nudged her. "No hanky-panky in my house."

She rolled her eyes. "Sweetie, the last thing your house inspires is hanky-panky." She pulled him down the hallway.

They all chatted while Brian fed the kittens. Adam had brochures about kitchen design, so that kept them busy and added authenticity to his claim that Marley was helping him plan the room. They agreed on clean, simple styles for the counters and cabinets. Marley sighed over a high-end stove. He'd have to save up for that, but maybe if he got a good end-of-year bonus …

They finally got Kari and Brian out the door. Marley and Adam collapsed against each other, overcome by giggles.

"I'm sorry," Marley said. "I honestly didn't invite them, but I couldn't figure out how to uninvite them."

Adam snorted. "It's okay. Kari told me I had to take you out tonight. You can be my wingman, and I can be yours, she said."

This set off another round of giggles.

Marley straightened and dabbed at her eyes. "Okay, I'm going to change."

"Change?"

She grabbed a large shoulder bag he hadn't noticed sitting near the door. "I thought it might look odd to wear a skirt and heels over here to talk about kitchen design. Back in a minute." She glanced at him over her shoulder. "Wingman."

Marley returned fifteen minutes later wearing a long-sleeved shirt in a deep turquoise color. It had a scooped neckline, and her long floaty skirt swirled about her knees. She'd let her hair down. It curled around her face and spilled over her shoulders.

"Well?"

He'd been staring. He met her gaze. "I'm not sure if I want to take you out so everyone can see you with me, or keep you here so no other guy can lure you away."

She laughed. "You're full of it, but thank you."

"I mean it, you look incredible. I don't often see you in a skirt and heels. Not that you have to dress up to look beautiful. You always look great–"

She held up a hand. "Don't tie your tongue into knots. I only meant you're full of it for saying other men would try to lure me away. I can't remember the last time someone hit on me."

"Are you kidding? I witnessed it myself a week ago, when Jamar and Luis were flirting with you here." Not to mention his own invite for this date.

She dismissed Jamar and Luis with a toss of her head. "They don't mean anything serious by it."

"How can you be so sure?"

"A woman knows."

Now she was the one full of it, because she certainly didn't know he'd been in love with her for a decade. But since this was clearly too soon to be throwing out the L-word, he kept quiet.

Adam had asked around for the best karaoke bar, since singing in public wasn't something he did. He drove to a quirky place with a tiki bar vibe. It was still fairly early, so they easily found a table to the side of the small stage with the karaoke setup. The waitress seated them and passed out menus.

"I'm told the mai tais are not to be missed," Adam said, "and they have good appetizers if you're hungry."

"You know, I could eat something. I was too nervous–" She broke off and looked sheepish, as if she'd revealed something she hadn't intended to share.

"I'm glad it wasn't only me," he said.

She smiled brightly. "It's silly, isn't it? We've known each other for years, ever since, well, ever since we were both a lot younger. Spending an evening together shouldn't be a big deal."

Personally, he wanted it to be a very big deal, but he'd take things slow, give her time to get used to thinking of him as a date instead of a little brother.

"Sure," he said. "We'll hang out, have some fun. Eat a little, drink a little, and one of us can sing as much as she wants."

They ordered the pu pu platter of mixed appetizers, plus mai tais. One drink would give him the excuse to stay there with her for at least two hours so he could sober up before driving home.

He certainly didn't want to get Marley drunk, but a drink might help her relax and lose some of her nerves over being out with him, over singing to an audience. Come to think of it, maybe he shouldn't have suggested as their first date an activity that could make her nervous. He didn't want her to transfer her anxiety over public performance to her feelings about him.

Oh well, too late now. She'd sing, or she wouldn't. He wouldn't push her any more than he already had. If she backed out, he wouldn't have to let her read his novel. He sort of wanted to know what she thought, but mostly he didn't want to risk her thinking it was lousy.

They chatted about the kittens, the café, the recipes she was testing, and what he could tell her about his work without breaking confidentiality clauses or boring her to tears. Mostly that came down to "I sit at a computer all day," but he had some funny stories about his coworkers.

The food came and between them they polished off the egg rolls, chicken wings, beef skewers, shrimp, and fried wontons.

"How does this karaoke thing work?" Adam asked. "I've avoided it, you will not be surprised to hear."

"You're not as bad as all that," Marley said. "I'm sure you're better than plenty of people who get on that stage."

"Maybe, but I'm not anxious to prove that tonight. Or drunk enough to make the attempt."

"Okay." She wiped her hands on a napkin. "It's not crowded yet. There's no line for the karaoke machine. I might as well do this now. Then we can either flee to hide my embarrassment, or else you won't drag me away from that thing all night."

"I won't complain either way."

She took a minute to warm up her voice by humming scales. Adam could have listened to her do that for an hour.

Marley went to the karaoke setup and studied the song list for a minute. Once she'd made a selection, she picked up the microphone and stepped onto the low, tiny stage.

A piano trill raced up the scale and back down. Other instruments joined in a grooving beat. Marley started singing "I Will Survive." Over the first half minute, her voice went from tentative to more confident. Her stiff posture relaxed. Her skirt swirled around her knees as her hips swayed. She didn't prance and posture for the audience, but she had started having fun.

Adam couldn't stop grinning.

When he managed to drag his gaze away from Marley, he checked on the rest of the audience. At one table, two women had turned toward the stage and were clapping along, their shoulders moving to the beat. A couple cuddled in a booth, watching Marley with smiles. A group of drunken guys at the back of the room quieted long enough to stare blearily at the stage.

The song paused for a moment. Her voice seemed to linger on the air.

The beat picked up again as she sang about being left, refusing to crumble, and still having love to give.

Had she chosen this song intentionally for its lyrics, or had she simply thought it would be fun? It made a suitable anthem. As far as Adam knew, Brian's father had never walked back through her door. No one even mentioned his name. But the rest of the song, about surviving abandonment, must have echoed some of her feelings.

Marley sang about saving her love for someone who loved her. Was she simply reciting the lyrics? Or could she really mean it? Could she be talking to Adam?

He couldn't stop the bubble of hope rising in his chest.

The song finished. The audience clapped enthusiastically. The guys at the back whooped and cheered. The waitress paused to compliment Marley and encourage her to sing another one.

Marley grinned at Adam, and he gave her a thumbs-up. She'd passed this first challenge with flying colors. Granted, he was biased, and a karaoke bar audience might not have high expectations. Yet surely anyone could see Marley's talent. He'd bet his house she would win that contest.

She went to choose another song.

How would her life change if she won the singing contest, if she got to perform, if she had a shot at being a professional singer? Would she move to a different city with a better music scene? Would she figure out a way she could tour, maybe in the summers? Would she make money and buy a house for herself and Brian, one in great shape, without an orange kitchen and dingy flowered wallpaper?

If she realized how amazing she was, it would put her even farther out of Adam's reach.

She wasn't sure she wanted to do the contest. It would be easy to talk her out of it.

He shoved away the thought. He didn't want any temptation to hold Marley back. She deserved whatever she wanted. Even if that wasn't him.

All he could do was make the most of this one night, and whatever other time he got to spend with her. For a decade, he'd been dreaming of a date with the woman he adored. He had that, and it exceeded his expectations. He wouldn't think any farther into the future.

He'd simply hold onto every opportunity he had to be with her.

Chapter 10

Marley's skin heated under the stage lights. Except the lights weren't that bright or that hot. The warmth came from Adam's gaze. His focus didn't waver. His admiring expression said she was the best singer he'd ever heard. He really was full of it, but she appreciated the generous support.

The music flowed through her. Singing felt so good, like letting out some part of her that usually stayed buried. Maybe at one time she had dreamed of fame and riches from a singing career, but there had always been this too. The simple joy of feeling her voice work, of hearing the sounds reverberate through the room.

She glanced at the other customers. Several kept their attention on her. A few couples had gone back to talking, and one rowdy group of guys in the back were more interested in drinking. One made a ribald joke, loud enough that she could catch a couple of words, and the others laughed uproariously.

Were they talking about her?

Her voice wavered. She stopped swaying.

She couldn't let that kind of thing distract her. She had to focus on the music.

This was why she didn't want to perform in public. You couldn't please everybody. Logically, she knew she shouldn't try.

And yet. When people ignored her, when they laughed at her –

Don't think about that. A professional would not only ignore it, but dismiss it so completely she'd forget it had ever happened.

Could Marley ever be that professional? That's why she liked singing to her son. He loved to hear her sing because he loved her. It didn't matter if she missed notes or forgot lyrics. It was nice that her family wanted her to be successful, certainly better than the alternative, but sometimes she simply wished they would leave her alone.

Still. It did feel good to sing.

The song ended. People clapped. Even the drunk guys in the back paused to cheer and whoop. She gave a tiny curtsy.

"Great stuff," the waitress said. "Do another? Please, keep those guys in the back off the stage."

Did she want to keep singing? Maybe she did. Maybe she should, whether she did or not. That's what a real singer would do.

She checked out the song options. She didn't recognize a lot of them. She hadn't been paying much attention to popular songs of the last decade, for some strange reason. Others she knew by name, but she wasn't sure of the tune, let alone the lyrics.

She found "At Last" by Etta James. An old song for sure, but she knew the tune and it had simple lyrics she could easily follow. It showed off the voice well too.

The music started with weeping violins. Twenty seconds later the first lyrics popped up.

It took half a minute to get through the first stanza. The words were happy, about finding love, but the pace made the song seem more like a funeral dirge.

She completely lost the guys in the back, and the women who had been bopping along to "I Will Survive" restarted their conversation. She hadn't remembered how slow this song was. It worked when you were listening and singing along while, say, doing the dishes. In a bar on a Saturday night, where customers were trickling in looking for the silly fun of karaoke, it bombed.

Lesson learned. Know your audience, and direct your choices to them. Things she'd have to think about more if she wanted to win that contest, or simply not embarrass herself during it.

Oh well, on this night, she only faced Adam and a handful of strangers. She wouldn't worry.

People clapped afterward, but not with as much enthusiasm. The waitress smiled but didn't push her to stay onstage. Adam lounged back as if he could listen to her all night, but that wasn't really fair to him, since they were on this weird date or whatever it was.

In any case, Marley had faced the public, albeit a small one. She'd had enough.

She slid in next to Adam.

He touched her forearm. "Fantastic. I hope you know how good you are."

She shrugged. "It wasn't so bad."

One of the rowdy guys stumbled toward the stage, calling for "Bohemian Rhapsody." He was too drunk to even pronounce the name right.

Marley grimaced. "But it may get bad soon." She swallowed the last of her mai tai. "What do you say we get out of here?"

He glanced at his empty glass. "Sure, but I shouldn't drive yet. Shall we go someplace else?"

She had to raise her voice over the off-key bellowing from the stage. "Any place where we don't have to listen to that."

He left money for the waitress and they fled the bar.

"Hey, I don't know how you feel about this, "Adam said. "Jamar mentioned his jazz trio is playing tonight."

She hesitated. Did she want their friends to see her out with Adam? Of course, she no longer had to worry about word getting back to Kari and their mother, since Kari had encouraged this outing. No one knew it was a date, so as long as Marley didn't act like she was on a date, their secret should be safe. Jazz wasn't a favorite of hers, but it would be interesting to see how they kept the crowd engaged. Besides, she would like to hear Jamar and be supportive.

"Sounds fun," she said. "It's nice to get out of the house, to stop being a mother and a daughter and a sister for a while."

He leaned closer. "You are so much more." His voice rumbled down her spine and sent electric sparks out to her fingertips.

She hoped he didn't notice the way she shivered.

Adam glanced at his watch. "They should be starting soon, and it's only a few blocks away."

"For you, maybe." She held out a foot. "I'm wearing heels."

He laughed. "Want me to carry you?"

"I do not." Her face, and other parts of her body, heated at the thought. She kept her tone light. "But between heels and that mai tai, I might have to hang on to you." She held her breath waiting for his reaction.

He winged out his arm. She slid her arm through his. He put his other hand over hers and tucked her close to his body. She felt warm all over. That had certainly been a powerful mai tai.

He took small steps so she could keep up without hurrying. They got smiles and occasionally a "hey" from the young people headed out for their evening entertainment. Marley thought a few of the guys were checking her out, and she knew some of the girls checked out Adam.

Fortunately, their town's entertainment district, such as it was, was clustered within a few blocks. They got to the club in less than ten minutes. Marley let go of Adam's arm as the guy at the door checked their IDs.

She shouldn't be embarrassed to be out with Adam. He was a great guy, and she wasn't the only one who thought he was cute, based on the glances he'd been getting.

Still, she didn't like rumors. She'd had enough of those her senior year of high school, when her pregnancy had started to show shortly after Christmas. She'd finished out the school year, but she had not enjoyed it. Some people she'd considered friends back then still greeted her with sympathy laced with superiority, even the ones who had divorced and become single mothers like her.

Would they change their tune if she won the contest? If she went on to do something with her singing?

Probably not. When people wanted to look down on you, they managed to do it even if they had to climb a ladder. She would always be the girl who got pregnant in high school, whose lover disappeared. She'd never prove herself to them. And what was the point of trying? She liked her life. Maybe it seemed boring to outsiders, but it suited her, and she'd never trade her son for anything.

This club was already more crowded than the karaoke bar, no doubt due to the men on stage. Jamar's trio might or might not be better than Marley, but they were definitely better than the drunk guy's attempt at singing Queen.

As they found a table, Jamar greeted them with a grin and a jerk of his chin. Marley smiled back and waved. Maybe she wasn't so boring after all, going out on a Saturday night with a cute guy, visiting two different bars, even knowing another cute guy in the band. See, she could still party with the best of them.

A waitress came by to take their order. Adam asked for a cola. Should Marley do the same? She was still feeling the last cocktail. But she'd been a waitress and knew the disappointment when the customers ordered cheap drinks. Besides, hadn't she just claimed to be able to party?

Wine didn't seem right after the mai tai, so she asked for a rum and coke. She'd slip it slowly, and she didn't have to finish it if she felt it too much.

Marley smiled at Adam and settled back to enjoy the music. The guys were good, and fun. Their music wasn't distant and inaccessible, like some jazz she'd heard. They kept to songs that had a lively, bouncy beat, filling the room with energy. They seemed to improvise, to some extent, starting with a tune and following where it led.

Jamar patted and plucked at the upright bass. The deep reverberations sent a thrill through her. The piano player flung himself around with abandon. The drummer had half a dozen small drums – bongos? – he played with his hands. Marley found herself wanting to get up and dance. No wonder the crowds came.

The band shifted into a slower song. Couples immcdiatcly flooded the tiny dance floor. They must be regulars who recognized this song and liked the way it begged the hips to move.

Adam held out a hand and lifted his eyebrows. "Dance?"
"Sure, why not?"

He took her easily into his arms. A shiver of delight ran through her. Maybe that was the alcohol, or the rare feeling of a man's hands at her waist. She hadn't done this in years. She'd bounced around the living room with Brian, sure, but not slow danced with a man.

They didn't have much space to move, so they turned in slow circles. The drum beats throbbed up from her feet to her spine. The piano kept her hips and shoulders moving, and the bass caused everything to tremble and shimmer.

Someone bumped her from behind, knocking her against Adam. He tucked her closer. Heat pooled in her pelvis. Oh, this was dangerous. This was too good. She'd forgotten that a few drinks, and a man's hands, could lead to trouble.

The song drifted slowly to an end, the last notes lingering in the air, in her chest. Marley backed away from Adam and took a gasping breath. She'd forgotten where she was, who she was with, who she was.

Had Adam forgotten too? Would he suggest getting out of there, taking a drive, finding someplace to park?

He led her back to the table and leaned close to speak over the next song, another upbeat one. "They're really good."

"Yes." Marley slumped back. She'd been foolish. Adam wasn't Neil. He was her friend, almost her family. He wouldn't take advantage of her in the backseat of a parked car.

For one thing, he had his own house. A house with a comfortable bed.

She wouldn't think about that. The idea had probably never even entered Adam's head. He'd barely dated, he certainly wouldn't expect this friendly, casual, practice date to wind up with them in bed.

She had no reason to worry about it, to think about it. She glanced at the line of his throat and that sexy triangle exposed by his open collar. The image of unbuttoning that shirt flooded her mind.

She forced her attention back to the stage. She concentrated on the musicians. Mostly.

They listened to the music, chatting only occasionally for the next 45 minutes. The band took a break and Jamar headed for them. Adam stood so they could shake hands and slap each other on the back.

"Hey, man, you came!" Jamar turned and held both hands to Marley. "And you."

She rose and took his hands. He kissed her on the cheek. She hoped one or two of her high school classmates were somewhere in the audience, watching this.

"What did you think?" Jamar asked.

"You guys are wonderful. I'm having a fabulous time."

He squeezed her hands before dropping them. "Great. Hey, I have to hit the little boys' room, guzzle about a gallon of water, and get back up there. You going to stay?"

Marley glanced at Adam. His expression offered her the decision.

"I think I've had enough," she said. "You guys really are fantastic, but this is a late night for me. I don't work tomorrow morning, but I don't want to throw off my early schedule too much. During the week, I'm up by four-thirty."

"Understood. Thanks for coming. See you both soon." Jamar gave her another kiss on the cheek before trotting to the back.

"He's such a nice guy." Marley couldn't help teasing Adam a little. "And see, he didn't try to steal me away."

"Well, he only has a ten-minute break. I hope it would take at least half an hour. Shall we go?"

Another couple pounced on their table as they left. The streets outside were busier. The young and beautiful were only getting started, while she called it a night. Oh well, let them have the Sunday hangovers.

She tucked her hand through Adam's arm as they walked back to the car. Her ankles were getting tired from wearing the heels. They weren't even particularly high heels, but she'd gotten so used to comfortable shoes. That wasn't a bad thing.

They stopped by the passenger side of the car while Adam unlocked the door. Marley turned to him. "I had a wonderful time. Thank you for taking me out and being my wingman."

He chuckled. His breath warmed the space between them. The cool night air behind her contrasted with the heat coming off his body. She hadn't realized they were standing so close together.

"I hope we can do it again," he said. "Soon. Often. I love spending time with you."

His right hand found her waist. His left did the same.

He gazed down at her with an expression Marley had never seen from him before. Or maybe she had, maybe it had been there forever, mostly hidden, barely peeking out sometimes.

She felt too hot, too cold. Her body was too big for the space it was in. She was floating outside of herself. She was firmly locked in beneath his hands. Her hips heated under his touch. The warmth spread through her.

Her lips trembled open. "Adam."

He leaned down, his gaze caressing her face, lingering on her mouth.

She wanted more than anything for him to kiss her.

Something cracked open inside her.

It was too much. Too much feeling. Too fast, too powerful.

She couldn't do this. Couldn't.

"No."

His hands tightened for a split second and dropped away. He stepped back. "Sorry."

He opened the door for her. Marley slid in, trembling, grateful for the solidity of the seat, the privacy of the darkness.

Adam shut the door gently and rounded the car. He got in and started the car without looking toward her.

Neither of them said anything until he pulled up in front of her house.

"Is this okay?" His voice sounded odd, raw. "If your mom's up, she'll see the skirt and shoes. But Kari may still be at my place."

Marley swallowed, cleared her throat, found her voice. "It's fine."

"I can text Kari to check where she is."

"No, it's fine." Marley fumbled for the door handle.

"Marley." His voice asked her to turn back toward him.

She couldn't. She stopped with the door partway open and one leg out.

"I'd never intentionally do anything to hurt you," he said. "You're important to me. Whatever you want, whatever you need me to be to you, I'll try. If this was a mistake …" He paused for a long time.

Did he think it was a mistake? Did she? She didn't know, only that she wanted to escape.

The pain came through in his voice. "We don't have to do it again. We can forget it happened."

A sense of loss crept over Marley. Maybe he could forget it. She didn't think she ever would.

She couldn't say anything. She didn't know what to say.

She slipped out of the car and closed the door. She backed up enough to get a brief glimpse of his face, a solemn oval almost hidden by the darkness. She lifted her hand in a small wave.

Marley turned and fled for the house.

She slipped out of her heels as soon as she entered the house. She tiptoed down the hall to peek in on Brian. His soft breathing calmed her, helped her nerves settle. Her son always came first. She'd made that decision long ago, and she'd never regretted it. What would he think if he knew his mother had almost kissed Adam, his buddy, their old family friend?

Her life had been fine. Why did Adam have to change that?

She hurried to her room, dragged off her clothes, pulled on a sleep shirt. She listened for the front door as she quickly brushed her teeth. She made it into bed, with the lights out, before Kari came home.

Had Adam kept his promise to not tell anyone about the date? Or had she hurt him so badly that he'd unburdened himself to Kari?

No, if he done that, Kari would still be there, comforting him. Unless she'd come home to confront Marley.

Marley's door opened a crack. Kari whispered, "Marley?"

Marley closed her eyes tightly and tried to breathe slowly and evenly.

The door eased shut with a soft click. Maybe Kari had simply wanted sisterly gossip about a night out with a friend. Maybe she wanted to tear into Marley for hurting Adam. Either way, she'd given up for now.

Marley shouldn't have asked him to keep a secret from his best friend. That wasn't fair. See, dating had been a bad idea. Their lives were too intertwined, their relationships already complicated.

Those moments at the car, the passion, the almost-kiss, played through Marley's mind. What if she'd made a different choice? What if she'd allowed everything to change?

Marley almost wanted to tell Kari everything. Almost. But most of all, she wanted to forget that night had ever happened and go back to how things used to be.

Simple. Safe.

Chapter 11

Adam hauled on the strip of wallpaper, forcing it down. He'd completed three walls of the living room. His shoulders ached. His back ached. His fingers felt raw on top of their ache. His whole body hurt.

It wasn't quite enough to bury the pain in his heart, but it helped.

A knock came at the door. Adam dropped the strip of wallpaper. It curved out from the wall like a wave.

He took a minute to catch his breath. It wouldn't be Marley. She wouldn't come over to say she'd made a mistake. He had to give up that dream. And he didn't want her coming over to apologize, or worse, to explain all the reasons they should forget dating.

He got it. He didn't need salt rubbed in his wounds.

He hardly had the energy to take the few steps toward the door, so he stayed where he was. "It's open," he called.

The door swung in. Colin stepped through and looked Adam up and down. "You look terrible."

"Yeah." Adam used his forearm to push hair off his forehead. His hands were filthy. So was the forearm, but not as bad. "I didn't get much sleep last night, what with feeding the kittens. Decided I might as well get some work done if I had to be awake."

Colin strolled around the room, studying the bare walls and the piles of shredded wallpaper on the floor. "Kittens the only reason for your insomnia?"

Had Marley said something to Colin? Or to Kari, who had said something to Colin? Adam didn't have the energy to sort it out. "You want coffee? Soda, beer?"

"Sure. You have something too." Colin held up a plastic container. "Diane sent soup. You look like you need a break."

Colin was right, judging by how Adam staggered against the kitchen doorframe and practically fell into a chair. He'd have to catch up on sleep before going to work the next day. Or take a sick day, but that would only leave him more time to think.

Colin rattled around in the kitchen for a few minutes. He put a beer in front of Adam. What the heck, it was a few minutes after noon. Colin had even kindly twisted off the top. Adam wasn't sure he had the strength to do it.

Colin took a long pull on his own beer, studied Adam, and shook his head. "You look—"

"I know, I know, like something the cat dragged in. More like something five kittens have been dragging around."

"I was going to say, you look like a man in love."

Adam's mind went blank. He stared at Colin.

"Hey, I recognize the signs," Colin said. "Kari hasn't figured it out. She's used to thinking she knows everything about you, but I've seen the way you look at Marley."

Adam gulped beer to clear his parched throat. "Yeah."

He had kept his promise. He hadn't told anyone that he and Marley were on a date. She couldn't fault him if Colin figured it out. Or maybe she could, maybe she'd think he should have hidden his feelings better. He was too exhausted and heartsick to care.

That wasn't true. He still cared.

The microwave dinged. Colin got up and returned with a bowl of soup. He put it and a spoon in front of Adam.

"I know I'm breaking all kinds of guy stereotypes," Colin said. "It's true, a few years ago, I wouldn't have noticed. Maybe I started paying more attention to people after my injury. I was always waiting to see how they reacted to a guy with half his leg missing. Or maybe I paid attention because I was afraid you were interested in Kari. You two are affectionate, no question about that. That day we built the wall inside the café, I saw her leaning on you, and I wanted to punch something."

"Glad you resisted the urge."

Colin lifted his beer in a toast. "I've evolved. The more I watched, the more I noticed. You're affectionate and easy with Kari. You watch Marley. You look at her the way I looked at Kari, when I didn't know if I had a chance."

Adam couldn't think of anything to say. He stared at the soup. He wasn't hungry. Or was he? He tried a bite.

"Jamar stopped by the café this morning," Colin added. "He said you two were at the club, having a good time. Kari says you're not answering her texts. Marley's not answering questions. She doesn't look as bad as you do, but she's having a rough day too."

Adam dropped his spoon. "What's wrong? Is she okay? She didn't drink too much, did she?"

"Relax." Colin made a 'slow down' motion with his hand. "She's claiming a headache as an excuse for moping around and avoiding Kari's nosy questions. Or maybe she's waiting for Kari to drag it out of her, so she'll have an excuse to talk about it."

Colin shrugged and shook his head. "I honestly can't tell. Anyway, Marley is moping, Kari is trying to meddle, and Diane thinks food will solve everything. Brian wants to spend the day with kittens, but Marley is insisting he do something else."

"She's taking this out on Brian? That's not fair."

Colin took another drink. "Yeah, well, mom prerogative, I guess. She's not wrong that he's been obsessed."

"He's passionate about animals. How can that be a bad thing?" Adam took a couple of deep breaths. Maybe Marley would say it wasn't any of his business how she raised Brian. But Adam had known Brian literally since before the boy was born. If Marley wanted to go back to only being friends, that was fine. Adam could hardly insist otherwise. But if she tried to cut Adam out of Brian's life …

Adam couldn't bear it.

Would Marley force Kari to choose sides? And their mother? Of course they'd choose Marley. Adam could lose them all.

Where would he turn if he needed help, to talk, a hug? Growing up, they'd been his real family. His mother suffered from frequent migraines. She'd been too busy with work, and too sick the rest of the time, to do much more than survive. She pushed Adam to go into a field where he could make plenty of money, so he could take care of her.

She'd remarried three years back. Her husband made enough that she didn't have to work. With his health insurance, she even found some treatments that worked for the migraines. Adam no longer had to take care of her. But she didn't take care of him either.

Kari, Marley, Brian, Diane, they were his real family. He couldn't bear not seeing any of them.

"Don't stress about it," Colin said. "She'll get over it."

"Right. Yeah. Sure." Adam breathed. He took another bite of soup. Marley was the baker, but her mother cooked hot, comforting meals. She'd been feeding Adam for years. She hadn't stopped simply because he'd taken her daughter out and brought her back miserable.

Colin had a point. Marley was freaked out and upset because Adam had tried to kiss her. It was his own fault. He'd told himself to go slow. He'd pushed too far, too fast, and she hadn't been ready. He'd thought –

Never mind what he thought, how he felt when he held her close dancing, when she'd turned toward him outside the car. He'd been so busy thinking about how he felt that he hadn't seen how she felt. That was his mistake.

Marley wouldn't hold a grudge. Today, she was tired and upset, like he was. She would get over it. What had

91

devastated him was probably no more than an irritation to her. Things would get back to normal.

Normal sounded like a long, aching path. But still better than this.

Colin drained his beer. "You want help with the living room?"

"Really? Didn't you just come off a shift at the café? In fact, shouldn't you still be there, and Kari too?"

"What's the point of being owners if you don't get to set your own schedule? We went in for a few hours this morning. Kari claims she wants to give the baristas more responsibility." Colin grinned. "I encouraged her, since I want her to cut back on her work schedule. But really, she couldn't wait to get home and find out how Marley's night went."

"Sorry to disappoint her." Adam ate more soup. "It was fine. We had fun, mostly."

After a pause, Colin said, "But it wasn't what you expected?"

"No. It wasn't that."

"I'm not asking. I know you well enough to know you wouldn't have done anything offensive. If Marley's moping, and you're trying to kill yourself with lack of sleep and physical labor, then clearly something went wrong. That doesn't mean it's your fault."

"It's my fault. I misread the situation. I thought I saw what I wanted to see."

"Maybe you did."

Adam grunted. "Not based on her reaction."

Colin stood and stretched. "Women are complicated. This family, more than most. They're used to having only women around, and the kid. They don't realize that we guys sometimes need things spelled out in big letters. So, you going to take a nap, or are we going to work?"

Adam glanced at the clock. "I'm going to feed kittens.

You do what you want, but you don't have to help me here."

"It's either that or go back with all those anxious women and get interrogated about what we said. You deal with your kittens. I'll be hard at work in your living room."

Adam finished the soup. It felt like a hug from Diane. For a few more minutes, he simply sat. He didn't have the energy to move. After getting rid of Kari last night, he'd paced the house, swearing at himself, and then did a marathon writing session in between kitten feedings. He'd written what he thought might be a powerful and emotional scene, but he didn't have the nerve to reread it. Then he'd spent five or six hours stripping wallpaper. He should know better than to torture himself this way, but what was the point in going to bed, staring at the ceiling, and thinking about his mistakes?

He'd taken his shot, and he'd blown it. It wasn't romantic to chase after a woman who'd made her lack of interest clear. It was stalking. He had to get over Marley.

It would take him time, but he could do it. Someday, maybe he'd meet another woman he could love. For now, he had to help them all return to normal. It wasn't fair to drag everyone one else into this.

He wanted to message Marley and tell her to send Brian over, that she had no right to keep him away. But issuing a challenge was not the way to keep things calm. He'd already said he was sorry. He didn't particularly feel like issuing a longer apology, and he didn't think Marley wanted one. She tended to hide her traumas. She'd want to know that the next time they saw each other, it would be okay.

How did he let her know it would be okay?

He rose unsteadily and peeked in on the kittens. Some were getting restless, but he could take five more minutes.

He headed to his bedroom, where he'd set up a desk with his computer, since that was the only tolerable room in the house. He kept his email message short.

You don't have to read this if you don't want to, but we made a deal. You kept your end. Here's mine.

Without thinking about what he'd written in the novel, without worrying about what she'd think, without second-guessing anything – much – he attached the first draft of the first half of his first novel, and hit send.

He looked at the bed. Swayed toward it. Held himself back. He did need a nap. But the kittens needed food.

Half an hour later, Brian appeared in the kitchen doorway.

Adam beamed at him from his position at the table with Brownie in one hand and a bottle in the other. "Hey! Good to see you."

Brian lingered in the doorway. "It's okay I'm here?"

"Always. Any time. And I mean that literally. Of course, your mom probably wouldn't appreciate you sneaking out in the middle of the night to visit, but I will never turn you away."

Brian nodded. He went to the box of kittens. "They're getting so big." He grinned and picked up Sugar, the white kitten with specks of tan. "She wants to play. How many have you fed?"

"I fed Sugar, no matter what she claims. I'm almost done with Brownie, but you can do the rest. Have you thought about which one you want to keep?"

Brian put Sugar back. He filled the second bottle, picked up Cookie, and sat across the table from Adam. "He's littler than Sugar. Come on, Cookie, take the bottle."

Cookie seemed more sleepy than hungry, but at last Brian got the kitten lapping at the bottle.

"I still get a kitten?"

"Of course. That's what we agreed, right?" Adam still planned to keep two, but he wanted to let Brian talk him into it.

Brian didn't look up from his task. "Mom was being

94

weird today."

"Oh?" Adam wouldn't ask Brian to tell tales on his mother. But he wouldn't stop Brian from talking if he needed to speak.

"She said I shouldn't come over today. You might want a break from me, and I should take a break from the kittens." His chin quivered. "I don't want a break."

"Hey." Brownie had finished, so Adam set down the bottle and tucked the kitten in the crook of his arm. He went around the table and put his hand on Brian's shoulder. "You do not need to take a break from me. I do not want to take a break from you. Maybe your mom is the one who needs a break."

"Yeah? Okay." Brian looked up and managed to smile. "I thought you might be tired of me."

"Never." Adam knelt beside Brian's chair so they were face to face. "You're one of my best friends. I don't get tired of you. Neither do the kittens. They need you."

Brian nodded. His shoulder relaxed under Adam's hand. The boy turned his full attention back to Cookie.

Getting up was a lot harder than kneeling, but Adam put one hand on the table and managed to rise without dropping the kitten or collapsing. He helped Brownie "eliminate" and put him back in the box. Cinnamon Bun hadn't been fed, but the orange and white kitten lay curled in the corner, so apparently she wasn't in a hurry. Adam would wait and let Brian enjoy the feeding.

"When I'm done here, can I read more of your story?" Brian asked.

"You bet. I can't wait to hear any ideas you have." Adam leaned against the counter. It kept him from falling over in exhaustion. "Hey, you said your mom didn't want you to come over, but here you are. She does know where you are, right?"

"Yeah. She said that earlier. A little while ago, I don't

95

know what happened, she changed her mind. She said I could come if I wanted."

Marley must have gotten his message with the novel attached. She'd taken his peace offering. "Good. I'm glad."

Maybe going back to normal wouldn't be the end of the world.

Chapter 12

Marley wasn't at all sure she wanted to read Adam's story. He was spending enough time in her head as it was. But she was very sure she wanted everyone to leave her alone, so she said she had something to read. She got Brian out of the house, which made him happy, and it meant she didn't have to see him looking as miserable as she felt.

Why had she thought she needed to keep Brian away from Adam? He wouldn't hold a grudge against her and take it out on her son. He wouldn't tell Brian about their date gone wrong. But maybe he'd appreciate Brian's help. Given the need for kitten care, she'd probably been punishing Adam more than protecting him from annoyance by keeping Brian away.

She shut the door on Kari, sat on her bed, and started reading.

His writing was pretty good. Maybe not "ready for a bookstore shelf" good, but certainly "this guy can tell a story" good. Marley didn't read much science fiction, but she did read a lot of novels, mostly romance, and some of them were set in the future or on other worlds. She wasn't sure where the story was going, but Adam had two people dancing around a relationship. If he brought them together, he'd have a sci-fi romance.

Did he plan to give them a happy ending? Had he changed his mind after she'd rejected him last night?

She put aside her tablet after half a dozen chapters. She knew writers didn't only draw on their own personal experiences, but she was struggling to separate Adam from the book's male lead. It gave her too many feelings.

At first she'd been angry with Adam for wanting to change things. Over the course of a long, sleepless night, she'd realized something. For him, it wasn't a change. She didn't know when it had started, but his feelings had been there for a long time. She thought again of *The Princess Bride*. All those years, Westley had said, "As you wish," when he really meant, "I love you."

Adam hadn't asked Marley on a date for practice, or because Kari wanted him to drag Marley out of the house, or because he couldn't find anyone else.

Everything he did for her, and much of what he did for Brian, showed her how he felt. Showed her that he loved her.

Over the years, without thinking about it, she had half-dismissed him as a nice kid, as if being nice was almost a weakness. As if real men were the ones who swaggered and flirted outrageously and made her laugh. Not the one she could call in the middle of the night if her son was sick and she needed somebody to pick up medicine.

He loved her.

She had no idea what to do about it.

Last night proved they had chemistry. A lot of chemistry. She didn't remember sex with her long-ago lover being as passionate as that not-quite-a-kiss.

In some ways, Adam was perfect for her. Younger, yes, but still a mature adult. He had a good job. A house. Marley wouldn't have to go on any more stupid dates that caused her anxiety, with strange men who disappointed her. She wouldn't have to wonder how the guy would react to her son, because Adam knew and loved Brian. Adam was practically a member of her family already.

He was the sweetest guy she knew, and he would never hurt her if he could help it. Adam would be easy. He would be safe.

That wasn't enough. Maybe it could be enough for her, for Brian. It would be a step up in their lives. Brian would have a father, Marley would have a companion who cherished her, and they'd have a house with enough space. Her meddling sister and mother would be close enough, but not too close.

But that wasn't enough for Adam. He deserved to be more than a safe bet, financial security, an easy escape from living with her mother forever. He deserved someone who would love him as deeply and passionately as he loved.

Marley liked Adam, and she respected him, and she cared for him.

She didn't know if she could love him like that.

The idea was too new. She'd have to think about it. But not yet.

Now she'd think about his writing. Should she encourage him to do more with it, the way he'd encouraged her to do more with her singing? Or should she leave him alone, at least for a while? He might not want her pushing him right now. He might think she was exaggerating how much she liked the story to make up for rejecting him.

It didn't seem right to ignore him though. Letting someone read what you'd written must be at least as hard as letting someone hear you sing. As he had pointed out, she knew she sang well. She'd heard that from choir teachers growing up. She could see people's reactions when she sang. She didn't know if she was good enough to be a professional, but she knew she was good.

Had anyone encouraged Adam with his writing? His mother wouldn't have. With her, it was always, "Make good money," not "Do what you love."

Marley vaguely remembered Adam and Kari working on stories together when they were kids. She'd thought they dropped that as they got older and busy with other things. It was merely one of those things kids did for a while, like drawing comics or putting on plays in the backyard.

She'd been too caught up in her own teenage dreams of greatness to pay attention to his dreams. Then she'd been caught up in her baby, and trying to make a life for herself as an adult, to worry about the neighbor kid.

In the end, Marley sent Adam a message as simple as his to her.

Thank you for letting me read this. It's good. I can always count on you.

Feeling better, Marley lay down to take a nap.

The phone woke her. She stared at the screen. It was Adam. She didn't want to answer. He might try to apologize for the night before. He hadn't done anything wrong. She should have told him that.

It would be mean to ignore his call now, simply for her own comfort.

"Hello." She held her breath.

"Two of the kittens aren't doing well. We're going to the vet."

"The vet? Will she be in? It's Sunday."

"I called," Adam said. "Jenna will meet us there."

"You and Brian? Are you sure that's a good idea?"

"Yes. Do you want to come?"

"Yes. I'll be ready by the time you get here."

"Okay. Five minutes." He hung up.

Marley rubbed the sleep from her eyes. Her mind hadn't caught up to the change of plans. Adam had mentioned bringing Brian to the vet for educational purposes. But with sick kittens? What if the vet had bad news?

Adam sounded confident that it was the right decision. Did she trust him?

She thought about everything she knew of him and decided she did.

With only three minutes left, she found her shoes and hurried to the bathroom to splash water on her face and brush her hair.

Marley ran out to meet the car as it pulled up. Brian sat

in the back with the box of kittens on his lap, so she took the front passenger seat. After one look at Adam's grim face, she turned her gaze to the windshield.

She blinked back tears. His expression had nothing to do with her. He was worried about the kittens.

Marley fiddled with the bag on her lap. If only she could do something, anything, to make things better. "You okay back there, Buddy?" Since Brian was directly behind her, she couldn't see him.

"Yeah. But Mom, they're really sick." His voice wavered. "Cinnamon Bun and Cookie."

"They seemed okay last night. What happened?"

"We took a break. We were working on Adam's story. At the next feeding …" Brian sniffled.

Marley twisted around. She couldn't see much in the box behind her. "Try not to worry too much, Sweetie. They might only have a cold or something."

Brian's silence showed what he thought of that optimism.

"It's my fault," Adam said softly. "I wasn't paying enough attention. The other three have been asking to be fed first, taking more formula. I guess I was giving more attention to them without realizing it. I had trouble getting Cookie and Cinnamon Bun to take their bottles earlier this morning. I didn't think …"

Would she have noticed if she'd been there? She wanted to believe her mother instincts would have kicked in, that she'd have immediately spotted a kitten in trouble. Even if that was true, she couldn't prove it, and it made her equally to blame, since she hadn't been there.

"You couldn't know," Marley said.

None of them knew anything about fostering newborn kittens. Why were they even doing this? How would Brian stand it if one of the kittens died? If all of them died? It would break his vulnerable little heart into millions of pieces.

101

Why had Adam insisted on letting Brian help with the kittens? The adults could have done it without her son's help. They could have protected him from this.

It wasn't fair to let him love something and then take it away.

They pulled up at the vet's office. Marley jumped out and opened Brian's door. He carefully undid his seatbelt and swung his legs sideways. With his arms wrapped around the box, he slowly got out. Three of the kittens squirmed and mewed. The other two lay limp. They didn't necessarily look sick. They could simply be sleeping. But Adam wouldn't be so worried if they were only sleeping.

Marley turned away to hide her face. She dashed to the office door.

It didn't open. She pounded on it.

Moments later, a woman with long brown hair unlocked the door and waved them through.

"Sorry to disturb you on a Sunday," Adam said.

Marley wasn't sorry, not in the least. Not when lives and hearts were at stake.

"It comes with the job." The woman looked vaguely familiar, but Marley didn't have the mental energy to figure out if they'd met before.

"Jenna, this is Brian," Adam said, "and his mother, Marley."

"Hi, Brian, bring the kittens on back." Jenna headed around the counter to the back room.

"Shouldn't we wait out here?" Marley asked.

"We won't worry about following the rules in an emergency. Let me see what you have."

If they had bad news, or if, God forbid, one of the kittens died in the next few minutes, they would have an angry mama bear railing at them for exposing her son to this.

Brian held the box as if carrying a priceless treasure. He set it on a metal exam table.

102

The vet slipped on a lab coat and rubber gloves. She picked up the black kitten, Brownie, first.

Marley almost snapped that the other two kittens were clearly the sick ones, but Adam and Brian simply watched silently, so she held her tongue. Jenna ran her hands over the kitten, checked its mouth, and listened to its heart.

"This one's doing well." She handed it to Brian. "Hold him for a minute. We'll keep the healthy ones separate."

Brian tucked Brownie close to his chest. He bent his head and nuzzled the kitten's soft fur.

Cupcake got the same quick examination, and Jenna handed the black-and-white kitten to Marley.

She held the tiny, warm bundle in her hands. It wanted to climb up her sweater. She supported it as it explored. How could something so tiny and precious survive?

Jenna finished with Sugar. "Let's put them here, in this travel cage. You'll need a couple of these to transport them as they get bigger. I'll send you home with two that people donated."

That was a good sign, right? The vet thought they'd need two cages to carry all the kittens. They'd be taking the sick ones home.

But people had donated carrying cages because their own pets had died.

Pain stabbed Marley in the breastbone. Her mother was allergic to cats and dogs. They'd never had the burden of loving and losing a pet.

They'd been so lucky.

Marley hardly knew these kittens, and she couldn't stand the thought of losing one of them. Adam and Brian had spent even more time with them. How would they bear it?

She wished she hadn't come. That horrible person who left the box outside the café door should be shot. Why had Adam agreed to foster the kittens? He should have insisted the shelter take them. He should have distributed them

103

among his coworkers. Anything but this.

Jenna examined the remaining two kittens. Poor little Peanut Butter Cookie and Cinnamon Bun.

The vet leaned on the exam table and looked down at the kittens for a full minute. Marley got the impression Jenna was gathering her strength.

The vet looked up and addressed Brian. "You've done a good job with them. I can see how much care you've taken. Unfortunately, these two aren't thriving. It's called Fading Kitten Syndrome."

"Can you cure them?" Brian asked.

"It's not really a disease. It's a set of symptoms that tells us something is wrong. You noticed how lethargic they are – how they aren't playful like the others. They aren't growing as quickly. In fact, they may have lost weight."

She picked up Cookie. "They're dehydrated." She pinched a little of the kitten's skin, pulled it up, and let go. "See how the skin doesn't bounce back right away? That means he hasn't been drinking enough. And his gums are pale." She spread the kitten's teeth so they could see.

Why was she doing this? They knew the kittens were sick. The vet didn't have to show them all the signs.

"What about the other three?" Brian's voice wavered. "Will they get it?"

"I'll do some tests to rule out an infection, but I don't think these two are contagious. Probably the other three will be fine, but I can't make any promises. We don't always know why FKS happens."

Jenna stroked Cookie's head. "Sometimes when kittens are taken from their mother too soon, they don't thrive. You can do everything right, as you have done, but they don't survive."

How could she say that to him? Marley should have insisted Brian wait in the lobby. She wanted to drag him out now.

She knew he wouldn't go.

Marley put her arms around her son. "It's all right, Sweetheart. It's going to be okay."

He stood stiffly. "Can we do anything?" he asked the vet.

"We do have good news. They seem to be breathing normally, not gasping. They're not crying out in pain. They have a chance." Jenna leaned closer and looked into Brian's face. "A chance, but no guarantees. You understand that, right? We do everything we can. We fight hard. Sometimes we still lose. It doesn't mean you did anything wrong."

Brian sniffled and nodded.

Adam leaned his elbows on the table so he was closer to Brian's level. "We're not giving up, right? We're a team. Like Jenna said, we fight as hard as we can, for as long as we need. I can't promise you they'll get better, but I promise we'll do everything in our power to give them the best possible chance."

Brian sniffed again. He looked into Adam's face for a long time. He must have trusted what he saw there. He nodded.

Jenna gave the kittens an injection of fluid under the skin. That big needle looked horrible against the little bodies, but Cinnamon Bun and Cookie didn't seem to notice. Maybe they were too sick to care.

The vet gave them another carrying cage for the sick kittens.

"Shouldn't we leave the two sick ones here?" Marley asked. "Couldn't you take better care of them?"

Jenna turned her direct gaze to Marley. "I'm telling you honestly, I can't do any more than you have. They'll make it, or they won't. You're giving them all the love and care you can. I couldn't do any better here. I have too many patients, and five other fosters at my own home right now. The best place for them is with you."

Marley wanted to scream at her. *With someone, maybe, but*

not with us. Don't make him watch them die!

Jenna gave them additional instructions. Marley suspected the vet was simply trying to give them something to do, whether or not anything would actually help. Adam took notes. Brian pulled away from Marley and listened carefully. He thanked the vet.

As they walked to the car, Marley put her hand on Brian's shoulder. "Maybe we should keep the kittens in separate places. You can keep feeding Brownie, Cupcake, and Sugar. Someone else can take the other two, focus on them."

He hugged the box closer. "No. I want to do it. Jenna said it wouldn't hurt them to be together and it might help. They're friends."

Marley shot a helpless glance at Adam. He shrugged. "I think Brian has earned the right. Nobody loves these kittens more than he does. If anything can save them, that will."

"They're not … it's not … it's not that simple," Marley said.

Adam got in the driver's seat and twisted to look at Brian as Marley slipped into the passenger seat.

"You heard the vet," Adam said. "Whatever happens, it's not your fault. You can't save them simply by wanting to save them."

"I know. Sometimes people have to leave. Like Grandpa did."

The pain sliced through Marley again. A little boy shouldn't know such loss.

"That's right," Adam said. "Your grandfather loved you. He wouldn't have left if he'd had a choice. We wouldn't have let him go if we had a choice. Sometimes we don't get to choose."

Brian nodded. Marley couldn't think of anything to say. She couldn't have spoken if she'd wanted to. She spent the drive home facing forward, trying not to cry.

106

Adam drove to his own house. Good, they would drop off the kittens, and Marley would get Brian out of there. If he would go, since he seemed to like Adam better than her now, simply because Adam gave him kittens, and let him spend all his time with kittens, and took him to the vet as if he were like, like, an adult who could handle hard things.

He wasn't an adult. He was her baby boy. She would do anything to protect him. Didn't she know what was best for him?

They stepped into the house. Brian headed for the kitchen.

Marley stopped two steps into the living room and looked around. "What? What?" She stared at the walls, blank except for stripes left by old wallpaper glue.

"It was a busy day," Adam said. "Look, what if Brian stays here tonight?"

She turned her astonished stare to him.

He held up his hands as if to stop the flow of words she hadn't even started yet. "I know tomorrow is a school day. I promise, I'll make sure he sleeps. I think he'd feel better having the kittens close. It will give him a little bit of control, to know he's there if they need him."

"But what if one … What if they …" She couldn't even say it.

"What if one dies?"

He moved in front of her. She thought he might put his arms around her, but he didn't.

He looked into her face. "We can't control what happens. We can't make things turn out the way we want. We can only do our best, and hope for the best. He'll have to learn that someday."

"But not now." Tears pooled in her eyes. "Why now?"

He held out his arms then, and she fell into them.

"I know," he said, holding her tightly. "It hurts."

Chapter 13

They moved the kitten care center into Adam's bedroom. It meant going back to the kitchen to warm up the bottles, but it also meant one of them could sleep on the bed while the other stayed nearby. Once they had everything settled, Brian started on the extra feedings for Cookie and Cinnamon Bun, while Adam lay down for a nap. All the worries in his mind swirled for a minute – and he fell deeply asleep.

A song sung in a high, sweet voice pulled him back to the world. Marley, singing him a lullaby?

As his groggy mind focused, he knew it wasn't her. She had a rich alto. This was the clear soprano of a preadolescent boy.

The desk lamp lit the room with a pool of light. Brian sat in the office chair with two kittens wrapped in a fluffy blanket in his lap, singing to them.

Adam's heart filled with so much affection it hurt. He listened without moving until Brian finished the song.

Adam sat up, rubbing his eyes. "What time is it?" he croaked. "How long have I been asleep?"

Brian picked up Adam's phone from the desk. "Ten fifty-five."

"What? At night?" Stupid question. Outside the windows, all was dark. "You should have been in bed hours ago. I promised your mom."

"You needed to sleep," Brian said.

"Fair point. Still." Adam stood groggily. "Did you get dinner?"

"Grandma came over. We had soup. Mom came later, with my stuff. She looked at you sleeping."

A little unsettling to think Marley had seen him sprawled on the bed, probably drooling and snoring. Oh well, he wasn't trying to impress her anymore. At least not much.

"Give me five minutes to make myself a bowl of soup," Adam said. "You need anything?"

"I'm not hungry." Brian flashed him a glance. "But Mom brought cookies. Molasses."

"Did she now?" Adam grinned. Marley couldn't be too annoyed if she delivered cookies.

Adam heated a bowl of soup for himself and got two cookies apiece for him and Brian. "Your mom's molasses cookies might be my favorite," he said. "On the other hand, her oatmeal raisin also might be my favorite."

"My favorite is chocolate chip," Brian said. "And those other chocolate ones, earthquake cookies."

Adam nodded. "Those are both definitely my favorites."

Brian giggled. You can't have that many favorites."

"Why not? Cookies are good. Why should I have to choose?"

Brian finished his cookie. He smiled slyly. "Like the kittens. They're all my favorites."

Adam laughed. "Okay, brat. You got me. It's hard to choose a favorite."

It was tempting to tell Brian they could keep all five kittens, if they survived. It was tempting to promise anything that would make this day better. But five kittens, to become five cats, who would need care for the next one to two decades?

No. Besides, what if some didn't survive? Promising to keep all five, and ending up with only three, would always remind them of the loss.

"I guess we'll have to say eeny, meeny, miny, mo," Adam said. "But not now. Now it's time for you to sleep."

Brian sighed and went to brush his teeth without argument. Poor kid. He carried a lot on those little shoulders.

Adam could have used a few more hours of sleep, but instead he tried to coax Cinnamon Bun and Cookie to eat a little more.

Brian came back wearing pajamas with lion cubs on them. He yawned. "Grandma said to tell you she'll come back at six in the morning. She'll feed the kittens and take me to school."

"What about her allergies?"

"She said kittens are worth the sneezing."

"Smart lady. I'll take tomorrow off work so I can stay with the kittens all day, but getting a break will be nice."

"You'll really take care of them all day tomorrow?"

"You bet." He coaxed the orange and white kitten to take a few more drops of formula. "I can't take off more time than that right now, but we'll figure out a plan." He looked at the tiny bundles of fur curled together in the warm box. "If they can't have their mama, at least they get us."

Brian came toward the desk. Adam expected him to simply say good night to the kittens. Instead the boy threw his arms around Adam. "Thank you." He kissed Adam's cheek.

With a kitten in one hand and a bottle in the other, Adam couldn't hug him back, but he leaned into the hug. "No problem," he said. "We're a team."

"Yeah." Brian crawled into bed. "Good night."

"Good night."

The boy's breathing slowed at once. He must have been as tired as Adam had been earlier. As Adam still was, really.

Cinnamon Bun showed no more interest in the bottle. Adam tucked her in with her siblings and started the next feeding for the healthy kittens. He didn't dare lie down on the bed, or he might conk out again. Instead he sat in his

110

chair, caring for kittens, and occasionally glancing at the sleeping boy. Adam was exhausted, and yet oddly satisfied. Clearly he wasn't a loner. He needed people and animals in his life.

It seemed that he'd still have Kari, Diane, and Brian. Maybe even Marley as a friend. Most people weren't that lucky. Perhaps the disastrous date was a blessing. If he let go of his foolish desire for more, he could truly appreciate what he had.

Adam tried to imagine another woman in his life, in his house. It almost worked, in a vague and blurry way. Until he got to the kitchen. He could only imagine Marley there.

He'd have to rethink that kitchen. He liked the ideas they'd discussed, but he'd never get Marley out of his heart if he kept a kitchen designed for her.

Yet at the moment, imagining anything else seemed like ripping out part of his heart.

He had plenty of other rooms to renovate. The kitchen could wait. Maybe it would become a symbol of getting over her, of building a different life.

Could he use something like that in his novel? Not a kitchen, but the metaphor.

Adam yawned, checked that the kittens were snuggled together warm and cozy, pulled over his laptop, and began to write.

When Diane came in the morning, Adam used the break to shower. That wasn't the same as a nap, but it helped him feel somewhat alert as he and Diane shared coffee while she fed kittens and Brian got ready for school.

"I put a lasagna in your fridge," Diane said.

Adam's mouth watered at the thought. "You're my favorite person right now."

Diane chuckled, but Adam was only partly joking. How did she work a full-time job, handle social media at the café, help take care of Brian, and keep everybody fed? Mothers must gain some kind of superpowers when they gave birth.

"Marley will leave her shift early," Diane said. "She'll be here about noon, so you can rest. Of course, Brian will join her after school."

He'd have to move the kitten care center back to the kitchen. He wouldn't be able to sleep if Marley was in his bedroom.

"I need to go into work tomorrow," he said.

"That's fine." Diane paused, her nose twitching. She rubbed it against her shoulder. "We have a schedule worked out. Between the baristas and our family, we can give the kittens … the kittens …"

She let go of Brownie, grabbed a napkin, and sneezed into it. Fortunately, Brownie was interested enough in the bottle that he didn't move.

Diane wiped at her nose. "We can give them almost constant attention in the café office. I'll pick them up at seven-thirty tomorrow morning and take them in, if that works for you."

He could drop them off on the way to work. It would take some time to get the kittens and all their gear inside and settled, so he'd have to leave earlier. Diane didn't start work until 8:30.

He had told Brian they were a team. He had to remember that too and let others take their turns. He couldn't do this by himself, but he didn't have to, because he had family.

"Thanks. That will be a help."

"They can stay until the café closes," she said. "That gives whoever's on the night shift time to sleep for a few hours after work."

"Night shift? Isn't that me?"

"It was one thing when we thought you'd have three hours between feedings." Diane winked. "We were willing to let you suffer through that. But if these two are going to need more frequent attention, you can't possibly keep that up. We'll take turns. Colin is on tomorrow."

"Diane, you are a treasure."

She gave a Cheshire cat smile. "I know."

Brian appeared in the doorway. "I'm ready, Grandma." He looked a little tired, but not as if he'd fall asleep in class. He kissed each kitten, and then Adam, before leaving the room.

Adam walked them out. As they went down the hallway, Diane said softly, "You know, you're like a son to me."

"You're like a mom to me."

"For a long time, I hoped you and Kari ... You know."

"Diane–"

"Don't worry, I gave up on that long ago. Now she has Colin, and he's a dear." She stopped in the arch to the living room. Brian waited by the front door.

"I wanted to say that no matter what happens, you'll always be like a son to me." She kissed his cheek.

Did she know about his feelings for Marley? Or at least suspect? He wouldn't put it past her.

Brian was waiting, so they didn't have to discuss it more then. Adam hugged her, waved to Brian, and staggered back to his room.

Whenever he didn't have both hands full with a kitten and a bottle, he made notes on his novel, and he finally answered Kari's messages. He couldn't tell her everything, but he assured her he was fine, and the kittens were holding on.

His TV was in storage until he got the living room fixed up. Thank goodness for the Internet. He checked some dating sites. He even started a profile on one, but he couldn't get up the nerve to make it live. Maybe someday. Not yet.

It was enough to note that there were other fish in the surrounding sea. Several women seemed interesting and

113

attractive. All were a few years older than he was. Did he have a thing for older women? Was he transferring his feelings for Marley to them? Or was it simply that he had so little in common with people in their early twenties? They made him feel old and boring.

Going out with Marley had been fun, because he was with Marley, not because he loved loud bars or strangers singing karaoke. He wanted a home. Children, one way or another. He didn't care if they were his biologically, or step kids, or adopted. He simply liked having kids around. He wanted to have the kind of house where all the neighborhood kids ran in and out, as comfortable as if it were their own home. He'd been lonely as an only child with his mother rarely home. Maybe he was still trying to make up for that. Regardless, kids were very cool. He might have gone into teaching if his mom hadn't pushed him along more lucrative paths.

Maybe someday he would become a teacher. They must always need math and science teachers.

It was funny how letting go of his dreams of marrying Marley opened up so many other ideas for his life. Not better ones necessarily, but things he hadn't even considered. He'd been too wrapped up in that one dream.

It was too soon to make big decisions. He'd wait a while for that. But it didn't hurt to think about things.

He searched for writing groups. If Marley was brave enough to enter the singing contest, maybe he should take his creative outlets more seriously too. He might never get good enough to publish, but he could get better. He'd read books on writing, and listened to some podcasts, and even taken an online class. But it would be nice to have actual, live peers. Maybe they could critique each other. He was ready for that. You could only go so far on your own.

Adam's phone beeped an alert. He'd set an alarm for 11:40 so he had time to move the kittens and their things before Marley arrived.

He stood and leaned on the desk, yawning hugely. At least he was too tired to worry about their encounter, and he had a ready excuse for fleeing quickly. One night without sleep, and a six-hour rest the evening before, had not been enough to put him back on track.

He looked into the box of kittens. Tiny Cinnamon Bun curled in a perfect circle, reflecting her name. Cookie sprawled on his side, one paw twitching. Adam nudged him closer to the others and tucked the blanket over him. Cookie's side heaved in a sigh and he settled down.

They were worth the fatigue. They might not be thriving yet, but none had died. Not on his watch.

Maybe they could save them all, working together.

He unplugged the heating pad, tucked up the cord, and gently carried the box to the kitchen. He needed lunch, but the kittens started to squirm, and he wanted to give Cookie and Cinnamon Bun an extra feeding before the bigger ones demanded their turns. He started with Cookie.

A tap came at the front door, followed by a soft voice calling, "It's me."

"In here. The kitchen." His whole body had tensed. He forced himself to relax.

Marley appeared in the doorway with a tentative smile. "I didn't want to wake you if you were resting."

They looked at each other through several heartbeats. Adam had been wrong. Getting over her wasn't going to be as easy as he pretended. Everything in him cried out to go to her, take her in his arms, try that kiss again. Good thing he had a kitten squirming in his hand to keep him grounded in reality, or he might have been tempted to try it.

He didn't want to guess what he saw in her face. It might have been longing, but he'd been wrong before. It might be regret, or pity.

Cookie squirmed and let out a plaintive mew. Adam jerked his attention down. He'd moved the bottle away without realizing it. At least Cookie wanted the formula. That was a good sign. Jenna had mentioned feeding them with a tube if they wouldn't eat. He hated the idea of trying to put a tube down a tiny kitten's throat.

His own throat suddenly ached. He cleared it. "I'm giving the two sick ones extra formula. They don't eat as much at once, so we feed them more often. Then you can take over and start the full feeding."

She headed for the coffee maker. "Did you get any sleep last night?"

"Sure." Did she know he let Brian stay up past eleven? He didn't want to keep secrets, but he wouldn't volunteer the information. "Not enough, but I slept some. Brian's a real trooper with this stuff."

She poured coffee. Frowned and sniffed at the cup. Poured it into the sink, and followed it with the rest of the pot.

"Getting spoiled, are you?" Adam said.

She chuckled. "Add a fancy espresso maker to my wish list for when I win the lottery. At the very least, I can make a fresh pot of coffee. Do you want anything? I saved a muffin and a scone from this morning's hordes, and I brought more cookies."

She gestured toward a pink bakery box sitting on the counter. He'd been so busy studying her face, he hadn't even noticed her carry it in. Or maybe he was learning to tune out anything pink or orange.

He eyed the box with longing. "I should have real food first."

"Do you have any real food?"

116

"Absolutely. What, do you think I'm one of those guys whose fridge holds a six-pack of beer and some ketchup?" He grinned. "It holds the lasagna your mom brought. But I'll save that for dinner and make a sandwich for lunch."

"I'll get it."

She looked so right in his kitchen, even against the cringe-worthy orange background. So capable and comfortable, puttering about as if she owned the place. He imagined them on a weekend morning, chatting over coffee, making plans for the day. He'd make her breakfast. He was good at breakfast.

His heart ached like it was trying to push its way out of his chest and go to her.

Cookie lost interest in the bottle. Adam needed to control his feelings. What if the kittens felt his grief? Would it interfere with their hunger, their will to live? He wanted them to know only love.

He helped Cookie eliminate, snuggled him back in the box, and picked up Cinnamon Bun.

Marley put the sandwich and a glass of water on the table. "Let me do that. Use your hands for eating."

He passed over the kitten. He tried to do it without touching her, but the side of his palm brushed her fingers. She made a small noise, or maybe that was the kitten whimpering.

They both looked down at Cinnamon Bun. Marley hadn't seen her in almost a day. Adam didn't think she looked worse, but it was still a shock when you saw how tiny and vulnerable they were.

Marley got to work with the kitten and the bottle. Adam washed his hands and then devoured his sandwich. He was too tired to make conversation, but he couldn't stop himself from looking at her. The way a tendril of hair curled past her temple and kissed her cheek. The way her hands moved so gently and competently handling the kitten.

117

The sandwich was perfect, thick with meat and slathered with mustard, the way he liked it. She'd sliced it neatly on the diagonal. He never bothered to cut his sandwiches in two, but it was a cute touch.

Why couldn't they do this every day? Why couldn't they have this?

He finished his sandwich and drank the water. "I need a nap." His voice sounded gruff. "Call me if you need anything.

She flashed a smile. "I will."

But he didn't think she would.

Chapter 14

Tuesday morning, the restaurant reviewer returned to the café. Holly was in the big cat room cleaning up after the pre-work rush, leaving Marley to face him alone. She stiffened and her heart hammered. How should she act?

As she would with any customer. Polite. Friendly, if she could manage it.

"Good morning. How are you today?" She hoped he wouldn't ask how she was in return. It would be too tempting to say *Adequate*.

"Fine." He studied the baked goods in the cases. "I understand you often sell out of your muffins and scones in the morning."

"Yes, nearly always by ten a.m. They're very popular with our regular customers." *More than adequate*. She managed to keep the words inside her head.

"Who are your regular customers?"

Was he suggesting that no one would like the place well enough to return?

She kept her smile in place by sheer force. "Mostly people who live or work in the neighborhood. They stop by for coffee and breakfast before work."

"People stop by even if they are not going to play with the cats?"

Marley bit her lip to hold back what she wanted to say, that of course people came by specifically for the baked goods, because they were *fabulous*.

She'd be professional if it killed her. She'd even be honest. "Some of them will take fifteen or twenty minutes to sit at the counter here and watch the cats while they eat. A few have our monthly passes, so they can go in with the cats anytime without a fee, regardless of whether or not they've met the minimum food or drink price. If they only have five minutes, they can pet a cat at no extra cost."

He studied the board that listed their specials and mentioned the monthly pass. "Yes, an interesting concept."

"Other people simply get their food and go. Some of them come back on the weekend, maybe with family members, to play with the cats." No doubt the cats were a large part of the draw for many customers, even those who didn't stay to play. But they had other choices in the neighborhood too, and they still chose to buy her baked goods.

"I'll have one each of the apple strudel muffin and cranberry scone," he said.

Okay, he didn't find her baked goods horrible enough to avoid them forever. Maybe to him, adequate was a compliment. "For here?"

"Yes. And please have your barista make me a latte." His mouth moved in a way that might have been a smile. "The cat in the foam was rather cute the other day. Does she have any other designs?"

Oh, sure, he was going to give Holly a great review for her coffee drinks and fancy foam art, and call Marley's baking adequate.

She mentally shrugged and put his items on a plate. She even added a bonus. "Try one of our Chai Tea Shortbread Cookies too, on the house. I'll have Holly bring the drink to you." His food and drink were easily over the $10 minimum, so she didn't have to worry about asking him to pay if he wanted to go into the cat room.

He even put a dollar in the tip jar.

"May I ask you something?" Marley said.

He turned back toward her.

Marley shifted nervously. "When I saw you the other day, you asked if I knew who you were. I didn't then, but I do now. Why did you ask?"

120

"Ah. In my job, sometimes people try to make a good impression. I want to review a place as it is for the average person, not with special treatment. You looked so confused, I decided that must have been your usual friendliness." He nodded and headed for the cat room.

Well. Mystery explained.

He carried his plate to the big room, opening the door for Holly and greeting her as she passed by with a tub of dirty dishes.

Maybe the review wouldn't be bad after all.

Marley took off her apron as Holly entered the kitchen. "The restaurant guy wants a latte. Give him something fancy in the foam, but not the cat you did last time. I'm going to take my break with the kittens. Holler if you need anything."

"I like this kitten-feeding thing," Holly said. "It's a great excuse to take a long break."

"Yep. Feed them, feed yourself, snuggle some adorable kitties." Marley snagged a chocolate chip cookie dough cupcake that she'd just finished frosting. "This time I'm making sure I get to try one of these." She headed for the office.

They'd bought an inexpensive electric kettle, so they could warm the bottles without going back and forth to the kitchen. Marley started the kettle heating and mixed powdered formula into water. She nibbled at the cupcake while the kettle heated.

Cupcakes as a nine a.m. snack, especially with cookie dough frosting and a ball of cookie dough inside, were probably not doctor-approved. But they were vaguely muffin shaped, and everyone knew muffins were for breakfast. Besides, she'd had a strenuous few days. Stress burned lots of calories, right?

The morning rush had kept her occupied. Now she was glad to get away for awhile. She had so many thoughts. Why

121

had she expected baking at her sister's cat café to be easier than her previous work as a waitress?

The morning schedule suited her, and so did the baking, but her life had gotten much more complicated. The restaurant reviewer. The singing contest, which started in a few days.

Adam.

She shouldn't have kept reading his novel. It had seemed a natural thing to do, hanging out in his kitchen with the kittens while he slept, reading his story. It had been fine at first, enjoying a fun adventure with likable characters.

Then she got to the last chapter, the one he'd sent that morning. This wasn't simply storytelling. He'd poured himself into it. He wrote it after their date, and it was full of love, and longing, and hope, and heartbreak.

After she finished reading it, she sat at his kitchen table with tears pooling in her eyes. Good thing he hadn't come in then. She would have thrown herself at him, begged him to love her the way his characters loved each other, begged him to give the story a happy ending. She couldn't bear it if his characters didn't get to be together.

She might have been projecting her own feelings a tiny bit.

Marley picked up Cinnamon Bun and offered her the bottle. The kitten squirmed. Marley touched the nipple to the kitten's lips. "Come on, sweetie, you need this. Open up. I promise it won't hurt you."

The idea that one of the kittens might die still terrified her, but Adam had made the right decision, both in taking them in, and in insisting Brian have a chance to care for them. Since their visit to the vet, he wanted to become a vet. She pointed out that sick and injured animals would come in, and he wouldn't be able to save them all. He would have to put animals to sleep.

"I know, Mom," he said. "But I can help them while they're alive."

She didn't have a response to that. She hadn't been able to speak.

Cinnamon Bun's tiny tongue finally started lapping at the formula. Marley sighed in relief. "Good girl. See, it's not so bad."

Marley snuggled back in the office chair, one hand curled protectively around the soft kitten, her other forearm leaning against the edge of the desk to support the bottle. How had Adam managed to do this several times a night for the last week?

Adam seemed willing to drop any suggestion of dating. Was that convenient or tragic?

Or maybe he was waiting for her to take the next step. Every time she thought of kissing him, she couldn't breathe. She wanted to run. But when she thought of letting him go, of him moving on to another woman who deserved him, she felt so empty she wanted to cry.

How could he do this to her? Make her full life seem empty without him?

Why had it taken her so long to see him standing right in front of her?

She hadn't wanted to see. She'd been afraid. She'd claimed she was happy, she had everything she wanted in life. And she did have so many things. Her son. Her family. Work she enjoyed. She'd focused on that so hard she'd refused to see what was missing.

Not merely a man. She didn't want *any* man. As far as the average man went, she could take him or leave him, and preferably leave him.

She wanted a man like Adam.

He would put her first, her and their children, and he would see Brian as one of those children. He would never make her first son feel second-class. His heart was so open to love. To children, to the kittens, to her family.

To her. If she dared take the chance.

She was a coward. She hadn't taken chances in years. She'd been burned by a foolish mistake at eighteen, so she closed herself off. She was responsible, sensible, good, helpful, trying not to ask for too much or be a burden on others.

Adam would never see her as a burden. They'd share all the other burdens in life, supporting each other, and Brian, and any other children they were lucky enough to have. They'd have enough love left over to give to kittens and puppies and family and friends who needed them.

They would find so much joy. If she could do it. If she dared to take the chance, to reach out with both hands and grab what she wanted.

If it wasn't already too late. If she hadn't hurt him too badly, made him close off his heart to her.

She'd been a coward for so long. She didn't know how to change.

She put down Cinnamon Bun, re-warmed the formula while she helped Cinnamon Bun eliminate, and started feeding Brownie.

She had a chance to prove she had courage. That she was willing to try. To change, to take everything life offered. She'd been half-thinking she'd pull out of the singing contest. It was too scary, too risky, not for her.

But she would do it. If she could get through that, standing in front of crowds, being judged for her voice, for who she was and what she dared to want, then maybe she could take the next step too, and take what she wanted for her personal life.

Maybe she could risk her wounded heart again.

It was foolish to correlate the contest to her romantic life, the judges to Adam. They were not at all the same thing.

Logically, she knew that winning the contest didn't mean she won Adam's heart, or even that she had the courage to be with him.

Maybe she was using the contest as an excuse, to put off that step, to avoid making a final decision about Adam. She admitted she was a coward.

She didn't want to be one any longer, but she had to prove something to herself before she could commit to anyone else. The singing contest was her challenge to herself.

Brownie gave up on the bottle, so she helped him eliminate and put him back in the heated box.

Something scratched at the door.

Marley stared at it, frowning. No one came in.

The scratching came again, along with a trilling mew.

Marley pushed back her chair and headed for the door. She cracked it open and blinked in the dim light at the end of the hall. A shaggy gray form moved in the shadows.

"Merlin! Did you escape again?" She blocked the office door with her legs so he couldn't enter.

The big Maine Coon was not only large enough to reach door handles, but also strong and smart enough to turn them. They thought they could keep him contained in the cat room with the round door handle inside the door. Either he had now figured one that out, or someone had carelessly let him slip through.

He still had two more doors at the tiny foyer before he could escape the building, but someone needed to adopt this cat quickly. Someone with secure locks.

Merlin head-butted her calf.

"Yes, you're a sweet boy, but you shouldn't be out here. Come on, let's take you back."

He sat on his haunches and pawed the door with his front feet. Apparently he couldn't get through this door. Yet. But why did he even want to?

Mew, mew, mew!

125

Marley had never claimed to speak cat, but suddenly she knew exactly what Merlin wanted, as clearly as if he had broken out in human speech.

"You know the kittens are in there, don't you? Why are you interested in kittens?"

Merlin was a boy. He shouldn't have maternal instincts. Father cats weren't known for devoting themselves to childcare. But Merlin was especially patient with children, and he'd often cuddled up with Shadow. Maybe he missed his little kitten friend the way Brian did.

Marley hesitated. They didn't let people bring their own cats to the café, because of the risk of spreading disease. But the kittens should be safe for Merlin, since the vet had just checked them. And all the cats in the café had their vaccinations and a clean bill of health.

He looked at her with his big gray eyes. She gave in. "Okay, we'll try it."

She opened the door. Merlin trotted ahead of her. As she crossed the room, he hopped onto the office chair and from there to the desk. He put one paw up on the edge of the box and peered in.

Marley looked into the box from the front of the desk. The kittens mewled and squirmed. At least three of them did. Two were distressingly still and silent.

Merlin jumped into the box. He curled himself around Cookie. He snagged Cinnamon Bun by the scruff of the neck and dragged her to his side. With two kittens nestled close, and the others tumbling around exploring this new addition, Merlin closed his eyes and purred.

First Marley blinked back tears. Then she took a picture. She couldn't wait to show Brian. She had to post the photo on the café's social media streams. This would get dozens of heart eyes and comments of "Aw!"

Before she did any of that, she sent the picture to Adam with a message: *I think we have a volunteer nanny.*

Chapter 15

Adam looked down at Brian. "You going to be okay?"

"Sure." He held Cookie in a towel in his lap. The little kitten latched onto the bottle and suckled like he couldn't get enough.

Merlin looked up from the warming box and gave his trilling mew.

"I'm not talking about the kittens," Adam said. "I know you know what to do about them." He scratched Merlin under the chin. "Both of you. I'm sorry you're not going to hear your mom sing tonight."

Brian's hair fell over his eyes as he looked down at Cookie. Adam wanted to brush that hair out of Brian's face.

Brian's thin shoulders shrugged. "I get to hear her all the time. I'm happy other people get to hear her now."

"Yeah." Adam squeezed Brian's shoulder. "Okay, Buddy. Call if you need anything. My phone's on vibrate, so I'll feel it even if it's noisy in the bar. We're only a few blocks away."

"Okay."

Adam stopped in the doorway for one last glance around the kitchen. Brian had everything he needed for the kittens, plus more cookies than even a nine-year-old boy could possibly eat in an evening. Some people bought toys when they felt guilty about their kids. Marley baked.

They might have gotten Brian into the bar to hear his mom sing, but someone had to take care of the kittens, and Brian was the one person who would find that preferable even to Marley's big debut.

Adam had offered to stay home with him, and he still wasn't entirely sure how things had been arranged this way, but he couldn't complain. He wanted to hear Marley. He wanted to see her blow away the other contestants. He wanted to see the look on her face when other people clapped and told her how amazing she was.

She'd be on with about twenty other performers, and the top five would go to the finals next weekend. Marley would make the finals, no question. By that time the kittens wouldn't need such constant care, so Brian could attend.

"I'll lock the door behind me," Adam said.

"Okay!" Brian's tone said, *I'm fine, get out of here*. Maybe the thrill of being on his own, being the babysitter instead of the babysat, was part of the appeal of staying behind. Adam had stayed home alone a lot at that age. He and Kari ran wild in their neighborhood, spending hours away from the adults. Brian rarely went unsupervised, even though he was more responsible than any of them had been.

He wasn't really alone now. Merlin had been taking care of the kittens all week, and Cookie and Cinnamon Bun were no longer fading. They ate full meals on a regular schedule. They'd gained weight. Maybe Merlin couldn't feed them, but his solid, warm, constantly-purring presence clearly gave the kittens something they needed.

Adam locked the front door, triple-checked that his phone was in his pocket and on vibrate, and headed for the club.

Marley, Kari, and Diane had been there for an hour already. They didn't know how long everything would take, and they didn't want Marley rushing to make her slot. Besides, it only seemed fair for all the competitors to watch and support each other.

By the time Adam got to the bar, every table was filled. He tucked himself against the wall to one side of the door.

The woman on stage wore a skintight red dress that barely made it past her hips. She sang the last couple of lines of a "Give Me A Reason To Love" by Portishead in a husky, sultry tone, rolling her hips. At the end, she bowed, flashing her cleavage at the bar. People – mostly men – whooped and hollered. As far as her singing went, she hadn't been bad, but had she been good? With the little he'd heard, Adam couldn't say.

He scanned the room. Dustin, the afternoon barista, sat with some male friends. Symphony, who ran a place where people could go for painting parties, caught Adam's eye and waved. It was nice that so many people had turned out to support Marley. Or maybe they'd be here anyway, and Adam had simply met more of the community lately. He saw a couple of people he recognized from the writer's group he'd joined. As far as he knew, they'd never met Marley, although with her work at the café, and previously as a waitress, lots of people must recognize her.

Adam finally spotted arms waving at him from a booth along one side. He wove through the crowd. He doubted the bar was usually this busy this early, but with almost twenty competitors, each with family and friends to cheer them on, the bar had benefited from this contest.

Kari scooted closer to Colin to make room for Adam. "She hasn't gone on yet," Kari said. "I think we have three more people first."

Jamar, Holly, and Diane sat across the booth. Jamar said, "Some good acts so far."

"But not you?" Adam asked.

"We have our gigs. Not looking for more."

"What about the woman in the red dress?" Adam asked.

Kari elbowed him. "Caught your attention, did she?"

Holly raised an eyebrow and smirked.

Adam felt himself blushing and hoped it was too dark for anyone to tell. "I only heard the end of her song. I didn't have time to judge if she was any good."

"Decent voice," Jamar said. "Sure knows how to please the crowd, at least the dudes. I don't know if that's what the bar is looking for. They want to bring in couples, groups of ladies out for girls night. You bring in the ladies, you'll get the guys. The other way around doesn't work."

Adam hadn't thought about things from the bar's perspective. The bar's owners or managers were the judges. They might not give the prize to the best singer. It had to be someone who'd bring in customers.

A couple of young teen girls, possibly sisters, went onstage. They sang a lively country song, one playing a guitar and the other a fiddle. One of them actually yodeled.

They were good. Maybe good enough to have a future as musicians. Still, Adam didn't think country music was right for this bar, and he couldn't imagine their parents would want them doing a regular late-night gig. It was still nice they had a chance to perform, and the audience clapped enthusiastically when they finished.

A young man took the stage. If he was over twenty, he hadn't filled out enough to match his height. The MC introduced him and his song, "Cry Me A River" by Michael Buble. An ambitious choice.

Recorded music played. "Now ..." The boy drew out the word. Unfortunately, his voice wavered in a way that didn't sound intentional.

Jamar grimaced and shook his head a little. Holly seemed more interested in Dustin's group of friends than the stage. Kari and Colin whispered to each other. Diane kept her full attention on the singer, but even she couldn't keep the occasional small wince off her face.

As the kid bashed his way through the song, many members of the audience frowned and murmured to each other. The ambitious song choice made it obvious the guy couldn't hit the notes.

When the song ended, Adam clapped loudly. At least the kid had the nerve to get up on stage. He must not know he couldn't carry a tune. Adam hadn't known how terrible his voice was until he heard it played back to him. It sounded fine in his head.

Most people clapped, if without enthusiasm. Nobody was rude enough to boo. The boy left the stage smiling and joined a man and woman who might be his parents. At least he had a supportive family. Hopefully they supported him for different dreams too.

The next competitors, a trio, were much better singers. Maybe not exceptional, but they could carry the tune and keep the timing. One man and the woman had guitars. The other man had a bass guitar. They played a lively country-rock song that Adam didn't recognize, maybe their own composition.

The cloud clapped and cheered. When the trio ended, Jamar said, "Good stuff. They know how to please a crowd."

Kari's chin went up. "Marley's better."

Diane nodded loyally.

In Adam's opinion, Marley's voice was definitely better. Still, a trio had some advantages when it came to entertaining. They didn't need recorded music as background. They could trade off in taking the lead, giving each other little breaks. And their bouncy music kept people happy and didn't demand anyone's full attention. Perfect for a bar, when you wanted people to feel free to chat – and order more drinks.

Adam had seen Marley a few times that week, but always with other people around, taking care of the kittens. He knew she'd been debating which song to sing. Would she have music playing in the background, or depend on her voice alone? Would she choose something slow and somber, like that Etta James song, which had been fabulous but hadn't caught the audience at karaoke night?

For the first time, Adam worried for her. He'd been so sure she would win, because she was good. But she wasn't the only one who was good. Marley wouldn't vamp for the audience like that first singer had. She might not have the happy energy and confidence of the trio.

She was good, but would her talent shine *here*? He couldn't bear for her to feel embarrassed. What if she regretted ever entering the contest?

Adam wanted other people to see how amazing Marley was, but most of all, he wanted her to know.

And then Marley stepped on stage, and Adam forgot everything else. She looked gorgeous in a flowing skirt and a wine-colored top that warmed her skin even under the bright stage lights. Her hair hung loose, curling over her shoulders, with a sexy tendril caressing her cheek.

Adam's mouth watered at the sight of her, and when the waitress paused at their table, he shook his head without glancing up.

Marley started to sing "Man I Feel like a Woman" by Shania Twain. She sang without background music, without any kind of accompaniment. Her voice filled the room and people went silent. She started out quiet, a little hesitant. Then she picked up speed and volume. Soon everyone in the bar was moving along with the music, some even singing along with the upbeat chorus.

Marley tapped her foot and swung her hips in time to the music, but she wasn't trying to seduce the audience with her body. She simply used the happily flirtatious song to catch their attention and keep them involved. By the time she finished, Adam's grin felt like it would split his face.

He clapped and cheered.

Marley bowed. She straightened with a Mona Lisa smile. She knew she'd wowed them all.

Her gaze scanned the audience and found their table. Her lips parted and joy lit her face. She waved.

Adam had to remind himself that her expression wasn't for him alone. She was smiling and waving at all of them. She was happy at her success, as she should be.

He wanted her to look at him like that.

This night wasn't about him. It was all about Marley.

She headed for the hall they must be using as backstage. The MC announced a fifteen-minute break before the second half. Adam wanted to see Marley and congratulate her, but he hated to leave Brian alone for too long, especially that late at night. The boy must be getting tired.

"I'll go back and send Brian to bed," he said. "Marley can have my seat if she comes out."

"Are you sure?" Diane asked. "I don't mind missing the rest."

Adam slid out of the booth. "No need to set off your allergies. With the kittens getting bigger and Merlin there, the fur is noticeable. You stay and congratulate Marley, and give her a big congratulations hug from me."

Diane winked. "Will do."

Jamar slid out of the booth too. "I'll walk out with you and stretch my legs. My sciatica is acting up."

They wove through the crowd. "Sciatica?" Adam said. "Isn't that something old people get?"

Jamar punched him on the shoulder. "Nah, man, it's a back thing. Means I've been too active, if you know what I mean."

They stepped out into the cool night air. "It means you've been helping remodel my house too much," Adam said.

Jamar nodded. "Sadly, you could be right. Don't worry about it. I'll walk you partway home. The walking helps."

It felt good to get away from the crowded club. Even though smoking was banned inside, the air in the bar felt stuffy and dense with all the bodies.

"What do you think, honestly?" Adam asked. "Does Marley have a chance?"

"She has pipes," Jamar said. "Maybe the best voice so far tonight."

They walked another half block. "You don't sound

133

entirely convinced," Adam said.

"No, she's good. It's only that she didn't mean it."

"Mean what?"

"What she was singing," Jamar said. "She performed the song, but it wasn't in her heart."

"Okay." Adam couldn't remember the lyrics. They hadn't seemed to matter. "I wasn't paying attention to the words."

"Exactly. Neither was she."

Adam thought about that for another half block.

When they got to the corner, Jamar stopped. "Guess I'll turn back here. Don't want to miss anything."

"Wait a minute," Adam said. "Are you saying Marley should have meant that song?"

"No, I'm saying she should have sung a song she meant. It's like Whitney Houston. Woman had a voice. Maybe the best of her generation. But when she sang, you pictured her on stage singing to a crowd of thousands. You didn't see her singing to *you*."

"Whitney Houston was famous."

"Sure, she deserved it." Jamar rubbed a hand over his short hair. "I don't mean to criticize. It's personal taste. Some people care about the tune. If that's what you want, you choose that threesome, or maybe the twin sisters. Some people care about the voice. That's where Marley wins. Her voice is fantastic."

"And you care about … the heart?"

"Look, I'm just saying, if she really wants to shine, she needs to sing songs that mean something to her." Jamar turned back toward the club. "Later, man. Give the kid a fist bump from me."

Adam thought about Jamar's words the rest of the walk home. What would Marley sing if she sang from the heart? As well as Adam thought he knew her, he couldn't say. Had she really meant it when she was singing "I Will Survive" or the Etta James song? What would she choose as her anthem?

He found Brian yawning at the kitchen table. All the kittens were curled up with Merlin.

Brian gave Adam a sleepy greeting. "How was Mom?"

"Fantastic, of course. I didn't stay long enough to see who the finalists are, but I bet she's one of them. Come on, I'll walk you home and you can get to bed."

"Okay." Brian shuffled some papers into a neat stack, in a casual-yet-obvious way that suggested he wanted to call attention to the lined pages covered in writing.

"You been doing some writing?"

"Uh huh. Would you read it?"

"I'd be honored."

"Okay." Brian stood. "Not now. Later."

"Sure. We can talk about it tomorrow, if you want."

"Okay." Brian said good night to each of the cats.

Adam put an arm around the boy's shoulders as they walked out. "You know, I started going to a writer's group that meets at the library. You could come with me sometime, if you want."

"Are there any kids?"

"A girl who's about twelve, I think, and a teenage boy. You'd be okay."

"I don't know. Maybe."

"No pressure. You have a lot going on right now."

They both did. Adam had spent the day working on the remodel with Colin, Jamar, and Luis. He had kitten care, and his writing, along with the new writing group. He was spending more time than ever with Brian, and seeing one or more of the women in that family daily. All that on top of his job.

His life had changed. Maybe not in the way he'd hoped, with Marley. But he had friends, family, a community. He felt more a part of the town where he'd grown up than ever before.

He waited while Brian brushed his teeth and crawled into bed. Adam wouldn't have minded reading him a story, but it was late, and Brian's eyes closed at once.

"Good night," Adam whispered.

"Good night," Brian mumbled. "Love you."

Adam's heart seemed to squeeze and then expand. "Love you too."

Chapter 16

Marley pulled the baking pans out of the oven and set them on the stovetop. She arched her aching back to stretch it. "Whose idea was it to do fruit tarts?"

Holly answered with a raised eyebrow. She knew very well Marley had been the one to dive into a complicated recipe on a Monday, after making their usual morning treats.

Marley had felt like she could do anything. She'd made the finals at the singing contest. Granted, a few of the other acts didn't have a chance. Still, some of the competition had been impressive.

For next weekend's finals, she'd be up against four others. The country-rock trio playing their original songs would be the ones to beat. A hard rock cover band of five guys had been too loud for the small space, but they were good. Another female singer had a decent voice and a spectacular figure. She knew how to use her body and that husky voice in a way that had men's tongues hanging out. A husband and wife team had sung jazzy classics. Musically, they were excellent, although they belonged at a different type of club.

The twin sisters hadn't made the final five, but they received a special youth award, probably something made up on the spot. They were at least as good as a couple of the other finalists, in Marley's opinion, but the bar reserved the right to judge by its own criteria, which included choosing a winner who could play regular weekend gigs.

Marley slid the tarts onto cooling racks and leaned over to take a deep sniff. The tarts looked good, and they smelled great. Given the ingredients, including fresh fruit, sugar, butter, and cream cheese, they ought to taste good too. Marley wouldn't want to make these every day, but if the café started offering catering, they could probably sell something this pretty for $15 each.

Holly finished with a customer and turned back. "I'm surprised you had energy for a special recipe after your big night."

"I did not do a whole lot on Sunday," Marley admitted. "Mom wanted to throw a party, but I convinced her to wait until next weekend." Then they'd either celebrate her really big success, or comfort her after her failure.

She wasn't sure which sounded worse. Failure meant embarrassment, letting down her family, and finally accepting the death of her dreams. If she couldn't even win a small-town bar contest, she was too far from being a professional singer to get there with the time and energy she had.

But success meant a lot of hard work ahead. Could Marley manage late Saturday nights performing, and early weekday mornings baking? The evidence suggested she could – if she spent Sunday recuperating, instead of hanging out with Brian and catching up on chores. Reality had far more annoying practical aspects than dreams did.

"Thanks for coming out to hear me," Marley added.

"What are friends for?" Holly tossed the comment over her shoulder as she wiped down the steam wand on the espresso machine.

Marley stared at her. Holly saw her as that kind of friend? Outside of work friends? Would Marley go out to support Holly if she had an art exhibit or something?

She absolutely would. "Yeah. I appreciate it." Marley rotated her neck. The mixing and kneading did a number on the body. "Guess I'll take my break now. What do we have left in the case?"

"From the morning baked goods, we're down to one muffin. We have plenty of cookies and brownies."

"I should probably stick to my yogurt and banana anyway," Marley said. "I thought I'd get tired of all the sweets, but it hasn't happened yet, so I suppose I'll have to attempt to exercise self-control."

"You win the contest and get a regular singing gig, you'll be up there working your booty under the hot lights. Plenty of exercise." Holly wiped down the counter, her back to Marley. "Would you quit this job if your musical career took off?"

Marley pulled yogurt from the fridge and sat at the table. "I haven't really thought about it."

That wasn't entirely true. She'd thought about it a lot, but mostly daydreaming about becoming successful and famous. She also had waking nightmares about becoming successful and famous, and destroying Brian's life with the crazy schedule and exposure to an edgier lifestyle. She hadn't considered the question for real, because the possibility seemed so unlikely.

Now it felt a little closer. Less of a fantasy, and more of a dream she might actually achieve with tons of hard work and a major dose of luck.

Marley looked around the kitchen. "I'd miss this. Maybe not the sore feet and tired muscles, but I'd have those on stage as well. I'd miss the early mornings, so quiet with nobody else here yet. I'd miss the smell of the baking. The satisfaction of doing something with my hands. Seeing something wonderful come out of my work. Happy customers whose day is a little bit better simply because I made something yummy."

Holly turned and leaned on the counter. She studied Marley with a solemn expression. They would never have gotten to know each other if they hadn't worked together. Their age difference wasn't big, merely enough that they hadn't overlapped in high school, but everything else about their lives separated them. Marley wouldn't have gravitated toward someone with such a goth look. She'd originally thought Holly was unfriendly and cynical.

After weeks of working together and seeing Holly with customers, Marley knew the truth. Holly was cynical, although about what, Marley hadn't decided. She was also incredibly kindhearted, clever, and a lot of fun. She didn't seem especially happy, but she tried hard to make other people happy.

"I'd miss you," Marley said.

Holly smiled, one of her rare, sweet smiles that slipped past her defenses. "I'd miss you too."

She turned away quickly.

Footsteps clattered down the hall. The kitchen door swung open and Kari burst through.

She stopped short, stared at Marley, and squealed.

"What?" Marley sat up straighter, her heart racing. "What is it?"

Kari held up a newspaper, shaking it so much Marley couldn't possibly see what was in it.

"A review! We're a hit! You're a hit!"

Marley slumped back, her limbs suddenly weak and numb. The paper had announced the contest finalists on Sunday. They'd been enthusiastic about all of the finalists but hadn't called out Marley in particular. No doubt they'd had to delay the printing to even get the finalists' names in the brief article.

Wait. Kari had said, *We're* a hit. *We*, not just *you*.

"The café?" Marley asked. "Did that guy finally do his restaurant review?"

Kari slapped the newspaper down on the table. Holly joined them to stare down at it.

"We'll start with the restaurant review," Kari said. "He spent the whole column on us. He said playing with cats he didn't know was surprisingly satisfying."

140

She ran her finger along the text as she read highlights. "We've created a happy environment that brings joy to everyone who enters. And! And! The baked goods are *sublime.*"

Sublime? Marley wasn't sure what precisely that meant, but it sounded a whole lot better than *adequate*.

"He talks about some of the things he tried. And then, look here."

Marley couldn't possibly look with Kari's hand waving over the text.

"He says, 'The only difficulty is in deciding whether to go early in the morning, to get one of the delectable scones or muffins, or later in the day, when the cookies and brownies reign. I recommend you make multiple visits, and especially try the five-item sampler. You won't be disappointed.'"

Kari started speaking in a rather pompous voice, with an accent that might have been an attempt at British. "I had my doubts about a cat café, and especially about any bakery associated with a room full of animals. I am delighted to say that Furrever Friends overcame all my objections."

Marley pressed her hands down on the table. She needed something to stay grounded. "He said that? That grumpy old man said all those things about me? I mean, us?"

Holly bent over the table and pushed Kari's hand aside. "Some of it's about us, but a lot is about you, or at least your baking. Makes sense, since he writes about food. Hey, he mentioned the foam cat I put on his latte." She nodded with a smug smile. "I worked hard on that."

Kari flung her arms around Marley and squeezed. "I knew it! I knew this would be perfect for you. For us."

Marley felt lightheaded. She sucked in air.

The restaurant reviewer liked the things she made. He hadn't even tried her fancy tart.

Had she been making the tarts hoping he'd come back in, so she could impress him with something he'd expect from an elegant French bakery?

Maybe she had. Maybe she'd been trying to prove her adequacy. Apparently she hadn't needed to go to the trouble.

"That's not all," Kari said.

Marley touched her temple. "I'm not sure I can handle any more."

Holly slid the paper over and pointed to the last line of the article. "I assume you mean this – 'See the story about the singing baker on page one.'"

"The what?" Marley said. "Who – who's that?"

Kari squeezed her again. "You, silly."

Holly flipped to the front page. Sure enough, a picture showed Marley onstage at the bar. The headline said, "Cat Café Baker Purrs Sweet Tunes."

Holly frowned. "That's a little sappy. I wouldn't call your singing purring."

Marley shook her head, hoping some of the jumbled thoughts would shake into their proper places. It didn't work. "They probably focused on me so they could use those puns."

"So what?" Kari said. "Free publicity! You'd better double the baked goods this week. I'll bet we get a lot more people in."

Marley groaned. If she'd known that, she wouldn't have spent so much time working on the fancy tarts. Now she wanted to go home and put her feet up.

Kari started pacing. "I'll get Colin to come in early to bake. I'd better see if any of the baristas are available for extra shifts too. We may have to control access to the cat room. Some cafés only let in a certain number of people at a time. I didn't think we'd run into that issue so quickly." She pulled out her phone and started messaging.

142

"It's not a bad article, despite the headline," Holly said. "It mentions the coverage of the contest from yesterday, and it looks like they have individual profiles of the other winners inside, so it's not quite as unbalanced as it seemed at first. But yeah, I'd say they featured this here because of the connection to the restaurant review. At least they're both flattering."

"Uh huh," Marley mumbled.

Holly studied her. "You okay?"

Marley pushed back her chair and stood. "I can't – I need – I need to go … think. I'll be – I'll be with the kittens."

Kari started to say something, but Marley ignored her and pushed through the kitchen door. Behind her, Holly was pointing out the fruit tarts, distracting Kari. They said something about Instagram.

Marley would be in Kari's office, but she hoped her sister would understand that she needed a few minutes of privacy. Privacy, and cats.

Of course, they had a whole room full of cats, but that room had customers, people who might have seen the articles and want to talk about them. Come to think of it, some of their customers had already said congratulations. Marley had assumed they'd seen the Sunday paper and knew she was one of five finalists at the bar contest.

She needed to gather her thoughts and figure out what all this meant. She closed the office door and headed for the chair behind the desk. She collapsed into it, sprawling like an oversized rag doll. Merlin lifted his head to look at her and trilled his mew.

"Hey," Marley said. "Everyone okay in there?" She didn't have the energy to check.

Merlin gently picked his way to the edge of the box. He hopped out and stood facing Marley until she scooted closer and sat up.

Merlin climbed into her lap and curled up.

"You think I need you more than the kittens do? I guess that says something. Why do I feel so messed up?"

She was a success as a baker, and a success as a singer. She hadn't won the contest, and a flattering article did not guarantee that she would. But even if she didn't, the publicity could change her life. People would know about her dream. They'd ask about it. If she didn't do anything with her singing, they'd know she failed, or gave up. She shuddered at the thought of more gossip.

On the other hand, even if she lost the contest, the publicity should be enough to get her auditions at other bars and clubs. It might act as a stepping stone to a demo CD, to meetings with agents. She knew enough about entertainment to know that a good story counted for as much as talent when it came to making someone famous. "The singing baker" made a good story. The teenage single mother who recaptured her dreams a decade later made a good story too.

Her dreams were suddenly shockingly real.

"So why do I feel like everything's falling apart?" She didn't want to be a good story. That wasn't her. Brian wasn't something to overcome.

Merlin simply purred. Marley rested her hands on his thick fur and let his rumble wash through her.

After a few minutes, her heart slowed and she stopped feeling like a tower of blocks about to topple. She pulled the warming box closer and peeked in. Sugar lay sprawled on her back, her rounded white belly heaving with faint kitty snores. Brownie went up on his hind legs, trying to climb out of the box. His tiny pink tongue flicked out as he shrieked a high-pitched mew. Cupcake batted at Brownie's waving tail. Soon the two were wrestling.

Cinnamon Bun looked just like her name, curled in a snug circle with her tail across her nose. Her fluffy fur rose and fell with her breathing. She looked healthy and relaxed now, not limp and fading. Cookie blinked lovely blue eyes at Marley and gave an inquisitive mew. His tan and brown pattern was becoming more distinct. He'd be a beautiful cat.

Merlin stood and hopped back into the box. Apparently he'd decided Marley was okay now. He curled up next to Cinnamon Bun and the other kittens tumbled around him. Merlin closed his eyes and purred.

"You're right, Buddy. You know what's important. I guess I do too."

Chapter 17

Jenna finished examining the kittens. "You've done well. They all seem healthy and thriving. You can start them on solid food later this week. If they don't have any trouble with that, they'll be ready for adoption in a couple of weeks."

"Good job, team." Adam grinned and gave Brian a high five. Yet the boy's chin trembled.

"It's a good thing," Adam said gently. "We saved them."

He wanted to hug Brian, but he recognized the fragile bravery. Brian looked like he would cry if anyone was too sympathetic to him. He wouldn't want to cry here.

Adam gave the boy's shoulder a quick squeeze. "Now you know how your mom will feel when you go off to college."

Brian sniffled.

"You have a talent for animal care," Jenna told Brian. "If you ever want to volunteer here, we'd be happy to have you."

That got a smile from Brian.

Merlin looked up at Jenna and trilled.

Jenna put her hand on Merlin's head. "You also have a way with kittens," she said. "We could use you here."

Merlin pushed against her hand and purred.

"I don't know why Merlin hasn't found his forever home yet," Adam said. "Maybe he's been waiting for the place where he was most needed. He loves kittens."

Jenna frowned as she studied the big Maine Coon. "I've heard of cats and sometimes dogs who seem to have that instinct for taking care of sick or injured animals. Maybe he'd do well with one of our foster families who specializes in kittens."

"I bet he'd love that," Adam said. "But he's ours for at least another week."

They got the kittens and Merlin into carrying cases. Adam picked up a case in each hand and Brian held the doors open as they headed for the car.

"My friend Cassandra wants to take Brownie," Brian said. "She had a black cat named Chocolate who died last year."

"Cassandra lives a few blocks away, right? You'll still be able to visit Brownie. That's great. And it sounds like she needs a new feline friend."

"Yeah. I don't know about Sugar and Cupcake though. Mike wants to take one but his dad said no."

"So you've chosen the two we're keeping? Cinnamon Bun and Cookie?"

Brian nodded. No surprise that he'd chosen the two who had almost died.

Adam set the carrying cases on the trunk and fished out his keys. "You know Luis, the guy who helped build the inside wall at the café? He mentioned that his mom might be interested in a pair of kittens. If they go together, they'll have each other for company."

Brian touched the grill on front of one of the cages. From the inside, Sugar batted at his finger. "Where does she live?"

"I'm not sure exactly, but I don't think it's too far from us. I'm sure you could visit once in a while." In fact, Adam would make that part of the deal. Eventually Brian would lose some of his attachment. He'd have two kittens of his very own to pamper. But it would be easier for him to let the other kittens go if he knew they had good homes, and he could visit them.

Brian chewed on his lip and looked sideways at Adam from under his thick bangs. "She won't let them outside, will she?"

"I didn't think to ask." Adam moved one of the carrying cases to the backseat. "Tell you what, we'll ask to do a home visit first. If you don't approve of her and the place, she doesn't get the cats."

Adam nudged Brian. "That doesn't mean you can put off letting the kittens go forever though."

"I know. I get why."

Brian opened the opposite car door. Adam slid in the second carrying case. The kittens pawed at the bars and meowed as Adam fastened seatbelts through the handles on top of the cages.

"Settle down, guys, we'll be home soon," Adam said. "We'll let them run around in the spare room now, the one we haven't started renovating. It won't matter if they have accidents, since the carpet will come out later."

Brian got in the front seat but twisted to look back at the kittens. "Do you think they'll miss each other?"

"I don't know. I'm an only child, like you. Your mom and Aunt Kari fight sometimes and tease each other, but I know they love each other too. Animals aren't exactly the same as us though. Some cats have particular friends, like Salt and Pepper at the café. Others are friendly with everyone, and some prefer to be alone. Huh, maybe they are like us, since people can be the same way. The kittens will have friends, whether other cats or people."

Brian was quiet as they drove back to Adam's house, but he shot occasional glances at Adam.

"Something else on your mind, Buddy?" Adam asked. "More than the cats?"

Brian looked away. "No."

"You know you can tell me anything, right? Trouble at school, trouble with a girl …" He raised his eyebrows and gave Brian a look.

Brian giggled. "No."

148

"You thinking about your mom this weekend? I'm glad you get to hear her this time."

"Me too." Brian smiled and wriggled in his seat. Maybe he was simply excited over the contest finals, or over getting to go to a bar with the grown-ups.

"Do you know what she's going to sing?" Adam asked. "Will she do the same song as last time?" He'd be happy to hear Marley sing that every day, but the judges might want to know that she had a larger repertoire. Patrons who came to both events might also prefer hearing something new.

"No," Brian said.

"Oh? What did she decide to sing?"

"I don't think she knows yet." Brian looked out the car window. He must have something on his mind, but if he wasn't ready to talk about it, Adam wouldn't pry.

As they pulled up to Adam's house, Brian said, "Can we work on our stories again?"

Ah, so that was it. Brian was still shy about his writing, but he was gaining confidence.

"Dinner and homework first," Adam said. "We always seem to run out of time on weeknights. But we can talk during the kittens feedings this evening, and maybe make some notes."

"Okay."

Adam smiled. He got plenty of time with Brian due to the intensive kitten care. They'd keep seeing each other after that, since Cinnamon Bun and Cookie would live with Adam. Lots of time to write stories together, and play with cats.

Unless Marley won the contest and used it to launch a singing career. Would that take her away from their small town to a bigger city? If she and Brian moved, they could take the kittens with them, since they wouldn't be living with Diane and her allergies. Adam could lose all of them – Marley, Brian, and the kittens.

He blinked to clear his vision. He'd be happy for Marley, if she had the chance to follow her dreams. He'd be happy for Brian and the kittens, if they got the chance to live together.

He'd have to be happy for all of them, since he wouldn't be happy for himself.

He remembered Marley singing "I Will Survive." He'd be the one trying to survive. Or maybe the appropriate song was "You Can't Always Get What You Want."

Kittens mewed in the backseat, and Merlin trilled at them. Adam pushed away his thoughts. He had no right to mope and feel sorry for himself. They'd saved the kittens. One miracle in a month should be enough for anyone.

They'd get the kittens settled back at home. Tomorrow, he'd get to hear Marley sing again. She would be amazing, and he'd savor every second. He couldn't wait.

Chapter 18

Marley knocked on Kari's office door. It was time to confess to her sister.

"Come in," Kari called.

Marley cracked open the door and peeked through. "Got a few minutes?"

"Of course. You feeling better today?"

Marley sat in the guest chair across the desk. "Yeah, I'm great. It was … overwhelming. I needed time to process everything." She peeked in the warming box, where all five kittens tumbled over Merlin and each other, wrestling. She recognized Merlin's long-suffering look from her own time with a toddler. "Feeding time?"

"Yeah, hand me those bottles and I'll mix formula."

Marley passed over the plastic syringes they used as bottles. How could she start this conversation? "So, about the other day. Sorry I fled and stole your office."

"Any time, you know that. Everything I have is yours."

Marley chuckled. "Including Colin?"

"If you want to borrow him to get the baking done, or for chores around the house, then sure. As for other stuff …" Kari narrowed her eyes in a mock ferocious glare. "Sorry, get your own guy." She started putting a rubber nipple on one of the plastic syringes.

Marley blew out a long breath. "I think I have."

The rubber nipple popped off and went flying. Kari's eyes widened. "Tell me everything."

"It's … it's Adam."

"Adam? My Adam?" The look on Kari's face was priceless. Marley might have admitted this earlier if she'd known how funny the reaction would be.

"You can't have both Colin and Adam." Marley bobbed her eyebrows up and down. "Unless y'all have an agreement I don't know about."

"No, I don't mean it that way, of course he's not mine like that. But …" Kari slumped back in her chair. She seemed to have forgotten the bottle in her hand.

"You really didn't know?"

"I knew he liked you, sure. For years. Teenage boy, gorgeous older girl. He always wanted to spend time with you." Kari looked at her hand as if surprised to see something in it. She took another rubber nipple from the supply box and fit it to the bottle. "I thought he'd grown out of it. I had no idea he still had that crush."

"It's not a crush."

"What do you mean? You were way too old for him. He had to know that."

"Not anymore."

"Well, maybe. But he'll get over it, I'm sure." Kari frowned. "Someday."

"Kari, are your feelings for Colin a crush?"

"No, but we're – oh."

"Adam is the same age you are. The age difference between the two of us is less than the difference between you and Colin. Adam is old enough to know his own mind. He's held these feelings for a long time, and he still feels them. Not a crush."

"Oh." Kari bit her lip. "Ah. What are you going to do?"

"I don't know. I have to figure that out." Marley crossed her arms and gave Kari a stern look. "You weren't trying to set us up when you insisted he take me out last week?"

"No, I was trying to get both of you out to be a little social, but not – hey, wait a minute. Are you saying that's when it happened?" She straightened and grinned. "That's when you two figured out–"

152

Marley shook her head and cut Kari off. "You don't get to take credit for this. We already had plans to go out. On a date."

Kari's eyes widened. "A date? Oh. You don't mean … a real date? You agreed? To go on an actual date?"

Marley didn't say anything.

Kari blinked, frowned, nodded, and finally said, "You're actually considering it? Him? Dating Adam?"

"I'm having a hard time thinking about anything else."

"Oh. Ahhh." Kari gave a sly smile. "That must've been some date. Tell me everything. Hey, why am I only hearing about this now?"

"It went … not badly, but …" Marley sighed. "You're right, I'd better tell you everything."

Kari filled the second bottle and they each took a kitten. Marley told Kari all about the events leading up to the date, and the date itself.

When she finished, Kari gave a satisfied sigh. "I love it. It would make me so happy to see you two together. Even though you kept secrets. My sister and my best friend. I can't believe you didn't tell me!"

Marley shrugged, refusing to feel guilty. "It was between us. We didn't want any meddling."

"I do not meddle!" Kari's smile turned sheepish. "Okay, I totally do. But only because I love you. And I'm trying to get better about only meddling when asked. So if I can do anything to help …" She sat up and gave Marley a look like a dog begging his person to throw a ball.

"I'm not sure what I need yet. I've known Adam forever, and yet this is completely new. It feels so weird."

"I understand," Kari said. "I feel weird about it too. But happy for you. At least I think so. Should I be happy for you? And for him?"

Marley concentrated on Cinnamon Bun, warm and soft under her hand, sucking on the rubber nipple providing life-giving formula. "I don't know. It's all so much. Everything is happening at once."

"Yeah. I can see why you were overwhelmed by the article. Okay, let's break it down. Take things one at a time."

Marley smiled to herself. She'd needed to tell Kari about this, because Kari deserved to know. Maybe she'd also wanted her sister's organizational skills. Kari would break down everything into pros and cons, and then make a detailed plan and schedule for how to get what she wanted. Marley tended to take life as it came. But right now, life was coming too hard and fast. She could use some planning help, as long as she stopped Kari from micromanaging.

"We'll start with Adam, because, well, because I can't think past that yet," Kari said. "Can you see yourself being with him? I mean, really being with him? Because, like you said, he's been into you for a lot of years. I'm not saying you have to make wedding plans tomorrow, but I'd hate to see him hurt worse, if he thinks he has a chance and he doesn't. He's pretty sensitive."

Marley stroked her thumb over Cinnamon Bun. Adam had saved this kitten and her brother. He'd gotten the failing kittens back on track, through sheer willpower, his determination to do whatever it took, and his willingness to follow through on that promise.

"He's stronger than you think," Marley said.

"Maybe." Kari frowned for a minute, then nodded. "Yeah. So you like him. He likes you. What's the problem?"

Marley looked up. "Brian."

"Why is that a problem? Adam and Brian have known each other for Brian's whole life. They get along great."

Marley sighed. "I wouldn't expect you to understand."

"Hold on a minute," Kari tucked Brownie back into the box and reached for Cupcake. "That's not fair. If you think I don't understand, explain it."

154

"Okay, right, I'm sorry." Marley put Cinnamon Bun in the litter box. Once the kitten did her business, Marley gave her a kiss. "Good girl."

Marley brushed hair off her forehead with the back of her wrist. "It's only that I've been raising Brian on my own for so long. It's hard to let someone else in."

"I know it's an issue when dating." Kari settled back down with the black and white kitten. "You don't want to bring someone into Brian's life, someone he might start to see as a father, and then kick him out again. Calm down, brat." She got a firmer grip on Cupcake. "It's feeding time, not playtime."

Back in the warming box, Merlin started grooming Cinnamon Bun, holding her with his front arms while he licked her face. The orange and white fluffball squeaked and waved her stubby tail.

"Isn't this a little different?" Kari added. "You know Adam would be there for Brian, even if the two of you broke up. Adam would never hurt Brian. And he'd make a fantastic father. Don't tell me you believe otherwise."

"I guess. I mean, I know he wouldn't hurt Brian, and he would be a great father. Still, there's something about taking that step. I've always put Brian first."

"I'd say you're putting him first if you date Adam. Brian wouldn't lose out."

"Maybe, but he's *mine*. Can I share?"

"Come on, how much does Mom help with Brian? How much did Dad do? You do share. Anyway, are you going to wait another ten years to start dating?"

"Ugh. No. That would be easier in some ways …"

She remembered the almost-kiss and went hot all over. She wanted that heat, that passion. And she wanted someone to hold her, to snuggle on the couch, to kiss her good morning. To share her fears and burdens.

"It wouldn't be better," Marley said. She picked up Brownie and started his feeding.

"Have you talked to Brian about this? Have you asked him how he'd feel?"

No, she didn't ask her nine-year-old son's advice or permission, especially when it came to men.

Maybe that was her mistake. Brian was old enough to stay home on his own. He was old enough to help foster kittens. She hated to admit it, but he was getting to the point where he didn't need her as much, at least in the same ways.

Sometimes she thought Brian was too old for his few years.

Marley rolled her eyes and gave an exaggerated sigh. "Okay, fine, you're right."

"I usually am," Kari said primly.

Marley resisted the urge to squirt formula at Kari. No need to waste it when Brownie was nursing nicely.

"Fine," Marley said. "I'll talk to Brian. I'll see what he thinks about me dating Adam."

"And if he's in favor of it?"

Marley felt like her insides were turning to champagne, all fizzy and tart. She couldn't breathe. Her vision blurred.

Merlin lifted his head and mewed.

Marley dragged in a breath. "All right, I'm all right. Yes. If Brian approves, then … we'll figure out the next step."

"Yay! I'll help. I'm good with next steps."

Marley might actually want the help. How could she go back to Adam and say she'd made a mistake by panicking and backing away? Had she hurt him too badly? Had she waited too long to make things right? What if Adam had given up on her?

Marley had to believe she still had a chance. But if they were going to move forward, she needed to let him know she was all in. She wouldn't hurt him again by taking one step forward and two steps back. Adam had offered his

156

heart. If she wanted to be with him, she needed to open hers.

Saturday night, Marley peeked into the bar. The place was packed, and she recognized many faces. Besides her family, and other friends from the café, she saw some people from high school. It seemed like everyone she'd ever known had reached out to her since the article. They'd been supportive. So supportive that even Marley's suspicious mind couldn't find ways to read between the lines.

Many messages started with, "I remember your singing." Some added, "I'm glad you're still doing it."

A lot also said, "I've been meaning to go by that cat café. I'll get there soon."

Several old acquaintances had come in the café while she was there, and she'd snatched a few minutes to catch up. The afternoon baristas also noted that a few people came in when she wasn't there. Some had left their numbers. She hadn't contacted anyone yet, and most she wouldn't. But one of the women had been a good friend. As Marley thought back on it, Gloria had never made fun of Marley, and Marley had been the one to cut ties. Maybe she'd limited her life more than she'd had to, and more than she'd realized.

Oh, well. She'd been young. So unbelievably young, it now seemed. She didn't regret her decisions. Still, it was time to move forward to a new life. A bigger life.

Everything she wanted seemed within her grasp. She simply needed to take it.

Her family came in and joined Jamar and Luis. Adam looked around but didn't spot Marley hiding in the shadows. She smiled seeing his tall lean frame, his hair that always seemed a little mussed, his clear gaze and sweet smile, and most of all, the way he put an arm around Brian and made sure he was comfortably seated with the best view. How had she been blind to these things for so long?

Brian looked around. When his gaze turned toward her, Marley took a step out of the hallway. She winked at Brian and wiggled her fingers. He grinned and waved back. They'd spent hours going over songs, trying to find one that said exactly what they wanted to say. In the end, they wrote their own. It was … adequate. For the tune, they'd adapted an old folk song, one with a happy, upbeat tempo. They'd managed to make the lyrics rhyme. She wasn't going to get famous or win any contests with it. But the message was true. That's all that mattered.

Brian understood what she was doing, and why, and he was 100 percent with her. He hadn't wanted her to sing because he wanted his mother to be famous, or popular, or rich. He'd worried that she wasn't living her life the way she wanted, that she wasn't following her dreams. He was smart enough to pick up on the idea that she'd given up singing because he'd come along.

He only wanted her to be happy.

The MC got on stage. Marley withdrew to prepare for her most important performance ever.

They started with the hard rock band. Their instruments were already set up on stage. It would be easier to pull them off stage when they were done than to get them set up during the middle of the contest. The band seemed even louder than the previous week. Marley was glad she'd given Brian earplugs.

The jazzy couple went next. After a short break, the country-rock trio played another original song. Then the sultry singer got on stage in a skintight, shiny red dress that made her look like Jessica Rabbit from *Who Framed Roger Rabbit*. Marley wasn't too happy about having to follow her, but at least they weren't competing for the same things.

Finally, the MC called Marley. She took a deep breath and stepped out on stage. She smiled at the table of family and friends. They all wanted her to be happy. She'd simply had to decide what would make her happy.

Now she knew. She only had to convince them this was it.

Marley locked eyes with Adam and started to sing.

I've known you forever, so how did I not see
That you knew me much better, and you are the one for me.

His grin faded into something more complex. He looked puzzled, maybe even wary. Had she waited too long to tell him how she felt? She'd gotten the courage to do this by believing she still had a chance.

Nothing to do now but keep going.

As she sang the next couple of verses, other audience members shifted and murmured to each other. Marley wasn't singing a familiar popular song, or something new destined to be an instant hit. She wasn't singing a song designed to appeal to bar patrons on a Saturday night.

It didn't matter. She spent too much time worrying about what other people thought and expected. This song was for Adam. Even if he'd changed his mind, he deserved to know how she felt.

You love all gentle creatures, from kittens to my son
Now I see into your heart and know you are the one.

Adam couldn't miss that. He shot a quick look at Brian, who grinned at him.

Kari had her phone out, filming the whole thing. She panned from Marley to Adam's reaction as Adam's smile returned, different this time. Not merely happy to hear her and proud of her. He was starting to understand that the song really was for him. He hadn't been sure at first. He'd been afraid to hope anymore. She'd done that to him.

But now she was giving his hope back, and answering it with her own.

She wanted to remember the look on his face forever. Maybe they'd share this video with their other children someday. She was starting to believe she could have that with him – a future, a family, a life filled with children and kittens and love.

Kari panned back to Marley in time for the final verse.

Can't imagine life without you. We would be so glad
If you would share our life with us, and be our kittens' dad.

Kari's shoulders shook in silent laughter as she tried to hold the phone steady. Their mom looked ready to jump up and hug everyone, bursting with happiness.

Adam put his arm around Brian's shoulder. The two males she loved more than any others in the world snuggled together and beamed at her.

Her family and close friends clapped enthusiastically as she bowed. The applause from the rest of the bar was more polite than enthusiastic, but she ignored the whispered comments and puzzled glances. Instead of heading backstage, she stepped down and squeezed between tables to get to Adam.

He shoved back his chair and stood. Marley went into his arms and lifted her face.

Now their kiss – that got some serious applause.

Chapter 19

Adam didn't want to let Marley go, ever. All his dreams had come true. He could stay in this moment for the rest of his life.

But slowly, reality crept in. They were standing in the middle of a bar full of people. Marley's son, and sister, and mother, watched them. Suddenly it felt as if everyone they knew, plus half of the town, stared at them.

Adam eased back.

The MC spoke from the stage. "The judges are conferring now. We'll have their answer in about fifteen minutes. Then we'll know who is the new bar star who will perform weekly under an eight-week contract to start. For now, order another round and enjoy yourselves."

The sound level rose about fifty decibels as people started chatting. Soon they'd have to deal with questions or congratulations.

"Can we find someplace quiet for a minute?" Adam asked Marley.

She took his hand and jerked her head toward the back hallway.

Adam paused and looked back at Brian. He lifted his hand and they bumped fists.

Adam grinned, his heart so full he could hardly contain it. He wanted to talk to Brian too, but first he needed a few minutes alone with Marley.

In the relative quiet and dark of the back hallway, they stood close together. "I don't get it," Adam said.

She put one hand on her hip and gave him a saucy look. "I don't see how I could have been more obvious. I had to write those lyrics myself, you know, with Brian's help.

They're not going to win any poetry awards, but we didn't leave a lot of room for misinterpretation as far as I can tell."

He chuckled. "No, I got that. At least, you really mean you want to …" He trailed off. Maybe he wasn't so sure after all. What did she want?

She slid both hands up his chest. "I want to be with you. I'm sorry I freaked out on our date. It's not because I wasn't enjoying myself. It's because it was going very, very well, and it scared me. I'm not scared now."

"So easy?" He put his hands on her hips. "Even before the date, when I hoped I might have a chance, I thought it would take months of sneaking up on you to get you to see me that way."

"I'm not quite so oblivious. I can recognize a good thing, when it stands right in front of me for about a decade."

He drew her closer. He dipped his head and her face lifted. Their lips brushed, tasted, paused, found each other again, like coming home.

Adam moaned with pleasure. He slid one arm around her back and rested his forehead against hers. He cupped her cheek. "I thought I had a pretty good imagination. It never came close to this. I'm going to have to go back and rewrite all the romantic scenes in my book."

She slid her hand behind his neck and up into his hair. "I'll help you research."

A few minutes later, they finally paused to breathe. "We should probably go back out there," Adam said. "Brian's waiting."

"That's one of the things I love about you," Marley said.

Adam's heart jumped at the word.

"You put my son first," she added, "even before you and me."

"I love him," Adam said simply. "Maybe as much as I love you, if in a completely different way." He smiled down at her. "You know, if you and Brian move into my house, he

162

can live with his kittens full time. That would make him very happy."

"Yes it would. We'll talk about that."

"Really? I'll hold you to that."

She pressed against him. "As long as you hold me."

A few minutes later, the MC's voice broke through their haze. They turned, arm in arm, and waited at the edge of the room so as not to distract from the MC on stage.

The man took several minutes to thank the patrons, the bar staff, and all of the musicians. Finally he got around to announcing the winner. The country-rock trio got the gig.

Marley clapped along with everyone else.

Adam looked down at her. "Are you okay with this, really? If you'd done a different song, you might have won."

"That's one of the reasons I didn't choose another song."

"You threw the contest?" He drew her back into the hallway where they could hear each other better. "Why?"

"I don't want to be a singer."

"But it's what you've always wanted."

She shrugged and shook her head. "Sure, at one time I dreamed of going on *American Idol*, making it to the final round, getting a contract, going on tour. At one point I also dreamed of being an Olympic figure skater or gymnast, even though I've only skated a few times and did a bit of gymnastics in grade school. The dreams we have as children are different from the life we want to live as adults."

"But you're good at singing. It's not only a childhood fantasy. You could actually be a professional."

"I honestly don't want to. I have work I love, family, friends, you. Nothing is missing. I think I enjoy singing more now because I'm not taking it seriously. There's no pressure. I can't imagine giving up what I have to devote myself to singing. It's not a trade I'd make, regardless of what happens between us."

163

"I want you to be happy."

She leaned into him. "I know. I am."

The trio played an encore song. People got up to mingle or leave. Adam and Marley headed for the door with the rest of Marley's family. On the way out, Marley paused by a table with several of the baristas, who offered their congratulations. Holly and Marley exchanged a high five and a few whispered words.

Outside the bar, they all paused in the parking lot.

Brian hugged his mom. "You were great."

"I got what I wanted out of tonight anyway," Marley said.

Adam held out his arms and Brian came in for a long hug. Adam kissed the top of the boy's head.

Jamar squeezed past another group to join them. "Now that was some fine singing," he told Marley.

She laughed. "Hardly. It was a silly song, but it said what I wanted to say."

"That's what I mean," Jamar said. "You sang from the heart, and it showed. You going to keep singing?"

Marley wrinkled her nose. "I don't want the hassle of being a professional singer. I'll never stop singing, I hope, but I don't want to worry about all the other stuff. This contest was good for me, but I don't think I'd do it again."

"I'll tell you what you want to do," Jamar said. "Come sing with our group sometimes."

"Your jazz trio?" Marley said. "You guys don't use a singer."

"We haven't had one. That's why we need you. We practice Sunday afternoons at Luis's mother's house. She has a big potluck dinner. All the kids and grandkids come, some cousins, some neighbors. I don't know who all, but they let me in so you know their standards aren't high. They have a big courtyard in the middle of the house, so there's room for the kids to run around and for us to play. Sometimes other people bring instruments and jam."

Jamar jerked his chin toward Brian. "Bring the kid. He'll have lots of friends to hang out with. Or he can sing along with us if he wants. It's a good time."

Marley and Brian looked at each other and seemed to communicate. "That sounds nice," Marley said. "I think we'd like to check it out."

Jamar punched Adam on the shoulder. "Bring this dude too. I'll text you the location. I'm gonna get back in there." He waved and headed inside.

Diane yawned. "It's late. I can take Brian home."

Adam and Marley exchanged glances. He felt that sense of communication. He thought he knew what she wanted. He definitely knew what he wanted.

"We'll take him home," he said. He put his arm around Brian. Marley did the same from the other side.

Diane beamed at them, as if seeing them together was a dream come true. Apparently, tonight's performance had only been a surprise for Adam.

"I thought you two might want some time together," Diane said.

"We'll have time," Adam said. He looked down at Brian, and then across at Marley. "We'll have a lifetime."

Dear Readers,

I hope you've enjoyed getting to know the gang at Furrever Friends. Some romance authors like to include an epilogue set a few months or years later, to show that the couple is still happy together. I've chosen not to do that here, but you'll see Marley and Adam together in future books in the series. Can you guess who's up next in book 3?

If you enjoyed these adventures, please leave a review on Amazon or elsewhere. Reviews help authors find an audience, and they help readers find great books.

I hope you'll keep an eye out for my future books. To learn more, please visit my website at www.krisbock.com or sign up for the Kris Bock newsletter at https://sendfox.com/lp/1g5nx3.

Turn the page to see the recipe for the Cherry Scones mentioned in this story. Then join my newsletter to get the rest of the recipes mentioned in this book and future cat café novels!

If you're interested in learning more about my home in the Southwest, visit my blog, "The Southwest Armchair Traveler" at https://swarmchairtraveler.blogspot.com/. I'll be sharing café recipes, Southwestern travel tidbits, quirky historical notes, and guest posts.

Kris Bock

Cherry Scones Recipe

This recipe also works well with dried cranberries or currents.

½ cup dried cherries, cranberries, or currents
apple juice or grape juice (about ½ cup)
2 cups flour
¼ cup sugar
½ tsp baking soda
2 tsp baking powder
½ tsp each salt and nutmeg
¼ cup cold butter
1 egg
½ cup plain yogurt (full-fat preferred)
1 tsp. lemon or orange zest

Preheat oven to 375°.
Soak cherries in juice for at least 10 minutes while you mix other ingredients.
Mix the flour and ¼ cup of the sugar. Blend in the baking soda, baking powder, salt, and nutmeg.
Cut in the butter with a pastry blender or two knives until the mixture has fine crumbs.
Stir in the egg, yogurt, and zest. Drain the cherries or other dried fruit well. Mix them in.
Spray a baking sheet lightly with oil.
Turn the dough onto the baking sheet. Pat it down into a 9-inch circle.
Cut the dough into 8 wedges. Separate them slightly. You may sprinkle with additional sugar if you want them to sparkle a bit.
Bake until golden and firm, about 20 minutes.
Serve warm with butter … or clotted cream, orange marmalade, or jam.

Sign up for the Kris Bock newsletter at https://sendfox.com/lp/1g5nx3 to get a free 10,000-word story set in the world of the Furrever Friends cat café.

You'll also get a printable copy of this recipe and the rest of the recipes mentioned in this book and future cat café novels.

Turn the page for a preview of *The Mad Monk's Treasure,* "Smart romance with an 'Indiana Jones' feel." It is always 99 cents or FREE with Kindle Unlimited! *The Mad Monk's Treasure* ranked 4.6 out of 5 stars with over 50 reviews.

Excerpt: *The Mad Monk's Treasure* by Kris Bock Chapter 1

Erin could hardly believe what she was seeing. Could this be it? After all this time waiting, searching, had she finally, finally, found what she was looking for?

She forced herself to sit back and take a deep breath. Don't make assumptions. Don't rush into things. She wanted to leap up and scream her excitement, but years of academic training held. Slow down, double-check everything, and make sure you are right!

She leaned forward and ran her fingers over the grainy photograph. With that one image, everything seemed to fall into place. This was the clue. It had to be.

She fumbled in her desk drawer for a magnifying glass and studied the symbols in the photo more closely. At a glance, they looked like your standard Indian petroglyphs. You could find them throughout the Southwest, tucked away in caves or scattered among boulder fields. She'd been on a hike just a few miles outside of town which took her past a wonderful series of handprints and spirals, and what looked strangely like a robot.

But this was different.

If she was right—and she had to be right—these symbols were a map. A map that could lead her to one of the greatest caches of buried treasure ever.

Erin flipped back a few pages, to the first photograph, the one that showed an overview of the boulder field. She confirmed that it had numbers identifying the specific rocks that the book then showed in detail. She could see a few outcroppings that would help orient anyone searching for those petroglyphs. The book also had a map of the area, and clear directions. She would be able to find the carved map. If the landscape hadn't changed too much the last century, anyway.

She pushed that thought aside, jumped up, and did a little dance. She reached for the phone. In a few seconds a voice said, "Yeah." Erin could hear the sound of some tool on metal in the background.

"Camie? I found it!"

The working sounds stopped. Camie said, "You'd better not be talking about that sweater you lost."

Erin laughed. "No, I found the clue! I know where the treasure is—well, at least, I think I've found the first clue that will—"

Camie cut her off. "Forget the disclaimers. You really found something? You mean, we might actually do this?"

The two women laughed into the phone together. Erin collapsed into her desk chair, her cheeks sore from smiling. "I'm so excited I can hardly breathe. Look, are you at work? I'll come by. I can get out of here in, oh, fifteen minutes, so I'll see you in half an hour?" She leaned over her desk and gazed down at the photo in the battered old book. "I want to show you where we're going. We need to make plans."

"I'll be here waiting." Camie's voice purred, with a touch of twang. "Honey, we're going places."

Erin hung up and gazed at the book a moment longer. Who would believe she'd found the clue to one of the most fabulous hidden treasures ever, in a battered old library book? The book must have been sitting there for years, quietly hoarding its secrets. But she had found it. Six months of research had led to this.

In the beginning, it had been a whim. Something to distract her from the tedium of teaching history classes at a small science college where students didn't value history. Researching lost treasures was fun, and she'd written a few articles about it for magazines. Reading the books on lost mines and buried treasures, you'd think the entire country was covered with them. The Southwest had more than its fair share, from miners who lost track of their remote gold mines, to prospectors who had buried bags of gold and never returned to retrieve them, to bandits who had hidden stolen loot and been killed.

But among all the legends, all the fact and fiction, one story stood out. The Victorio Peak legend had it all. A Franciscan priest and a swindler. Torture, murder, a government cover-up. Where was the truth, among all the stories? Erin wanted to find out. Over time, and with Camie's encouragement, she'd started to take the treasure hunt more seriously. It wasn't so much for the treasure itself—that would most likely belong to the government or the landowners. But from the start, she'd recognized the potential, should she ever unearth new information. Forget academic publications; this was the kind of story which could capture the general imagination and catapult her into success as a writer of popular nonfiction. It would make her reputation, open up new job opportunities—change her life in ways she hardly dared dream.

She touched the book gently. The pages were falling out; she didn't want to risk carrying it around. Instead, Erin snapped a picture of the petroglyphs with her phone. That would be enough to show Camie for now.

She put the book back on her shelf among the hundreds of others she either owned or had borrowed from various libraries. Then she flipped through her stack of topographic maps and found the right one in southern New Mexico. She tucked the phone and the map into the small waist pack she used when biking around town.

Her stomach rumbled, a reminder that she'd been so caught up in her work she'd skipped lunch. She forced herself to stop and have a bowl of cereal. She ate standing up in the kitchen while her mind raced through the planning of the treasure hunt. The timing was perfect; she'd made her students' final papers due the previous week, before finals. She just had to turn in grades and field a few tearful last-minute requests for extensions, and she'd be done for the semester. What better way to spend the summer, than hunting for buried treasure?

Erin shook her head. Who would've thought that she, the quiet, studious girl who'd spent her life in academia in one way or another, would be planning such an adventure?

She checked that the front door was locked, a habit left over from living in bigger cities, grabbed her bike helmet, and went out the back.

Erin wheeled the bike around the front of her house and mounted. At the corner, she paused and looked both ways. The long frontage road was dangerously narrow, with a cement wall on one side and a ditch on the other. Fortunately, traffic was normally light, and at this time of day the road lay empty. Erin pushed off, still grinning from her find. She rode on the right side, by the ditch, instead of facing traffic, because it was just too frightening to ride alongside the wall when a car passed.

She'd gone a block when she heard the hum of a car engine as it pulled out from a side street behind her. She rode along the very edge of the pavement, even though the car would have plenty of room to pass her without oncoming traffic.

Erin glanced over her shoulder. The black SUV 20 feet behind her hadn't bothered to pull out into the road at all. Jerk. When would drivers learn to share the road with bicyclists? Erin pulled onto the two-foot wide gravel strip between the pavement and the ditch. She couldn't stop without risking a skid, but she slowed so the SUV could pass.

The engine roared. Erin glanced back again.

Black metal bore down on her. Her heart lurched and the bike wobbled. This guy was crazy! She whipped her gaze forward, rose up in the seat, and pumped the pedals with all her power, skimming along inches from the ditch. He was just trying to scare her. She'd get his license plate and—

She felt the bumper hit her back tire. The bike seemed to leap into the air, and she went flying. The dried mud and weeds of the ditch seemed to rise up to meet her.

She didn't even have time to scream.

About the Author

Ordinary Women, Extraordinary Adventures

Kris Bock also writes novels of suspense and romance with outdoor adventures and Southwestern landscapes. *The Mad Monk's Treasure* follows the hunt for a long-lost treasure in the New Mexico desert. In *The Dead Man's Treasure*, estranged relatives compete to reach a buried treasure by following a series of complex clues. *Whispers in the Dark* features archaeology and intrigue among ancient Southwest ruins. *What We Found* is a mystery with strong romantic elements about a young woman who finds a murder victim in the woods. In *Counterfeits*, stolen Rembrandt paintings bring danger to a small New Mexico town.

Read excerpts at www.krisbock.com or search for Kris Bock on Amazon. Sign up for Kris Bock's newsletter at https://sendfox.com/lp/1g5nx3 for announcements of new books, sales, and more.

A legendary treasure hunt in the dramatic—and deadly—New Mexico desert....

The lost Victorio Peak treasure is the stuff of legends—a heretic Spanish priest's gold mine, made richer by the spoils of bandits and an Apache raider.

When Erin, a quiet history professor, uncovers a clue that may pinpoint the lost treasure cave, she prepares for adventure. But when a hit and run driver nearly kills her, she realizes she's not the only one after the treasure. And is Drew, the handsome helicopter pilot who found her bleeding in a ditch, really a hero, or one of the enemy?

Just how far will Erin go to find the treasure and discover what she's really made of?

Praise for *The Mad Monk's Treasure*:

"The action never stopped .... It was adventure and romance at its best."

"I couldn't put this book down. You'll love it."

"The story has it all—action, romance, danger, intrigue, lost treasure, not to mention a sizzling relationship...."

Counterfeits

Kris Bock

Painter Jenny Kinley has spent the last decade struggling in the New York art world. Her grandmother's sudden death brings her home to New Mexico, but inheriting the children's art camp her grandmother ran is more of a burden than a gift. How can she give up her lifelong dreams of showing her work in galleries and museums?

Rob Caruso, the camp cook and all-around handyman, would be happy to run the camp with Jenny. Dare he even dream of that, when his past holds dark secrets that he can never share? When Jenny's father reappears after a decade-long absence, only Rob knows where he's been and what danger he's brought with him.

Jenny and Rob face midnight break-ins and make desperate escapes, but the biggest danger may come from the secrets that don't want to stay buried. In the end, they must decide whether their dreams will bring them together or force them apart.

Praise for *Counterfeits*: "'Counterfeits' is the kind of romantic suspense novel I have enjoyed since I first read Mary Stewart's 'Moonspinners', and Kris Bock used all the things I love about this genre. Appealing lead characters, careful development of the mysterious danger facing one or both of those characters, a great location that is virtually a character on its own, interesting secondary characters who might or might not be involved or threatened, and many surprises building up to the climax." 5 Stars – Roberta at Sensuous Reviews blog

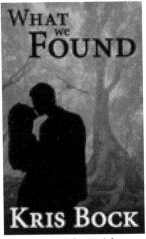

22-year-old Audra Needham is back in her small New Mexico hometown. She just wants to fit in, work hard, and help her younger brother. Going for a walk in the woods with her former crush, Jay, is a harmless distraction.

Until they stumble on a body.

Jay, who has secrets of his own to protect, insists they walk away and keep quiet. But Audra can't forget what she's seen. The woman deserves to be found, and her story deserves to be told.

More than one person isn't happy about Audra bringing a crime to life. The dead woman was murdered, and Audra could be next on the vengeful killer's list. She'll have to stand up for herself in order to stand up for the murder victim. It's a risk, and so is reaching out to the mysterious young man who works with deadly birds of prey. With her 12-year-old brother determined to play detective, and romance budding in the last place she expected, Audra learns that some risks are worth taking – no matter the danger, to her body or her heart.

Praise for *What We Found*: "This is a nonstop suspense. Love the characters and how real they seem with every episode played out."

"Another action-packed suspense novel by Kris Bock, perhaps her best to date. The author weaves an intriguing tale with appealing characters. Watching Audra, the main character, evolve into an emotionally-mature and independent young woman is gratifying."

"This book had me guessing to the end who was the murderer. Well written characters drive the story. Good romance. Exceptional and believable plot twists and turns. I loved it!"

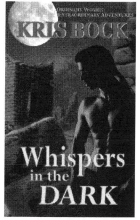

Young archeologist Kylie Hafford heads to the remote Puebloan ruins of Lost Valley, Colorado, to excavate. Her first exploration of the crumbling ruins ends in a confrontation with a gorgeous, angry man who looks like a warrior from the Pueblo's ancient past. If only Danesh weren't so aggravating... and fascinating. Then she literally stumbles across Sean, a charming, playful tourist. His attentions feel safer, until she glimpses secrets he'd rather keep hidden.

The summer heats up as two sexy men pursue her. She finds mysteries – and surprising friendships – among the other campground residents. Could the wide-eyed woman and her silent children be in the kind of danger all too familiar to Kylie?

Mysterious lights, murmuring voices, and equipment gone missing plague her dig. A midnight encounter sends Kylie plummeting into a deep canyon. She'll need all her strength and wits to survive. Everything becomes clear – if she wants to save the man she's come to love and see the villains brought to justice, she must face her demons and fight.

Whispers in the Dark is action-packed romantic suspense set in the Four Corners region of the Southwest.

Praise for *Whispers in the Dark*: "This book was a delight from start to finish!"

"Whispers in the Dark has a hefty dose of adventure and mystery, as well as a strong main character."

"This book kept me turning pages until the end. The plot was full of twists and turns, always keeping the reader rooting for the heroine. Excellent read!"

Children's books by Chris Eboch

Ms. Bock also writes for young people as Chris Eboch. Her novels are appropriate for ages nine and up. Learn more or read excerpts at www.chriseboch.com or search for Chris Eboch on Amazon.

The Eyes of Pharaoh, a mystery set in Egypt in 1177 BC, brings an ancient world to life. When Reya hints that Egypt is in danger from foreign nomads, Seshta and Horus don't take him seriously. How could anyone challenge Egypt?

Then Reya disappears. To save their friend, Seshta and Horus spy on merchants, soldiers, and royalty, and start to suspect even The Eyes of Pharaoh, the powerful head of the secret police. Will Seshta and Horus escape the traps set for them, rescue Reya, and stop the plot against Egypt in time?

The Well of Sacrifice: a Mayan girl in ninth-century Guatemala rebels against the High Priest who sacrifices anyone challenging his power.

Kirkus Reviews said, "[An] engrossing first novel…. Eboch crafts an exciting narrative with a richly textured depiction of ancient Mayan society…. The novel shines not only for a faithful recreation of an unfamiliar, ancient world, but also for the introduction of a brave, likable and determined heroine."

The Genie's Gift is a lighthearted action novel that draws on the mythology of The Arabian Nights. Shy and timid Anise determines to find the Genie Shakayak and claim the Gift of Sweet Speech.

But the way is barred by a series of challenges, both ordinary and magical. How will Anise get past a vicious she-ghoul, a sorceress who turns people to stone, and mysterious sea monsters, when she can't even speak in front of strangers?

Bandits Peak: While hiking in the mountains, Jesse meets a strange trio. He befriends Maria, but he's suspicious of the men with her. Still, charmed by Maria, Jesse promises not to tell anyone that he met them. But his new friends have deadly secrets, and Jesse uncovers them. It will take all his wilderness skills, and all his courage, to survive.

Readers who enjoyed Gary Paulsen's *Hatchet* will love *Bandits Peak*. This heart-pounding adventure tale is full of danger and excitement.

Haunted follows a brother and sister who travel with their parents' ghost hunter TV show and try to help the ghosts.

In *The Ghost on the Stairs*, an 1880s ghost bride haunts a Colorado hotel, waiting for her missing husband to return. *The Riverboat Phantom* features a steamboat pilot still trying to prevent a long-ago disaster. In *The Knight in the Shadows*, a Renaissance French squire protects a sword on display at a New York City museum. During *The Ghost Miner's Treasure*, Jon and Tania help a dead man find his lost gold mine—but they're not the only ones looking for it.

Pig River Press
Socorro, New Mexico
Copyright © 2019 Christine Eboch

Made in the USA
Middletown, DE
05 March 2021